STORM WARNING

LINDA SUE PARK

SCHOLASTIC INC.

NEW YORK TORONTO LONDON AUCKLAND
SYDNEY MEXICO CITY NEW DELHI HONG KONG

To Ginger Knowlton, who is never clueless.
—L.S.P.

A B C
D E F
G H I

J K L
M N O
P Q R

S
T U
V

W
X Y
Z

ISBN 978-0-545-34138-7

12 11 14 15 16/0

Printed in the U.S.A. 40

This edition first printing, May 2011

Book design and illustration by SJI Associates, Inc.

CHAPTER 1

"Bahamas."

"Jamaica."

"Bahamas."

"Jamaica."

Dan gritted and clenched every part of his body that could be gritted or clenched. He tried one more time. "BA-HA-MAS. Amy, think about it—"

"I *am* thinking about it!" his sister shot back. "Which is more than you're doing! Look, if we're going to go where *she* went, it has to be Jamaica. She wasn't even a pirate when she lived in the Bahamas!"

They were talking about Anne Bonny, who had disguised herself as a man and become a swashbuckling pirate way back in the 1700s. And who might—or might not—be one of their ancestors. In China, Dan had found a miniature portrait of a woman with Anne Bonny's name on the back. It was their only lead to the next step in their quest.

Amy and Dan were Cahills. For more than five

hundred years, Cahill family members had been among the most influential people in the world. Scientists like Galileo and Marie Curie; artists and writers like Vincent Van Gogh and Mark Twain; world leaders—Napoleon and George Washington; the list went on and on . . . and it was looking like Anne Bonny might have been a Cahill, too.

In the early 1500s, the Cahill family had separated into branches, each bearing the legacy of a child born to Gideon and Olivia Cahill. Oldest son, Luke: the Lucians. Strategists, politicians, businesspeople. Sister Katherine: the Ekaterina branch, innovators and inventors. Brother Thomas: the Tomas clan of explorers, adventurers, and athletes. And sister Jane: the Janus line, populated by artists and visionaries. Since that time, the factions had been battling one another in a desperate race to find the secret to becoming the most powerful people on the planet.

Amy and Dan had joined that race. Not that they knew what they were doing at first. When their beloved grandmother Grace died, the terms of her will gave them a hint toward the first Clue—and set in motion an adventure they could never have imagined.

Not alone, either. Other teams were chasing down the Clues, too—teams that would do anything to keep Amy and Dan from getting there first. Explosions, cave-ins, atttempts to poison them, drown them, bury them alive. In France, Austria, Japan, Korea, Egypt, Australia, South Africa, China . . . Dan and Amy had survived it all, finding several of the precious Clues along the way.

And they *still* didn't know what they were doing.

They were now in the Beijing airport waiting for Nellie, their au pair, who was at the currency exchange window.

"Jamaica was the last place anyone ever saw or heard of her," Amy said. She had already researched Anne Bonny online. "So that's where we should start looking."

"But—" Dan stopped, trying desperately to think of a way around Amy's reasoning. She was good at this stuff, at seeing the big picture. He was more a detail guy, and right now he was very interested in one particular detail about the Bahamas.

Amy looked him right in the eye. "I know what you're thinking, Daniel Arthur Cahill," she said sternly. "Don't be ridiculous. We've got to beat the other teams to the next clue. We don't have time to waste at some dumb amusement park."

Dan yelped. "'Dumb amusement park'? Is that what you think it is? Don't you know *anything*? Oceanus is the biggest water park in the world! They've got, like, a hundred waterslides! And you can swim with dolphins! And see stingrays and piranhas!"

"Ha!" Amy pointed at him in triumph. "I *knew* you were thinking about Oceanus!"

"Well, it's the last thing *you'd* think about," Dan said bitterly. "The only person in the world who has no idea how to have fun, and she has to be my sister. No wait, I take that back. Your idea of fun is a library open twenty-four–seven."

Amy's eyes widened in hurt. "D-Dan, that's not f-fair," she said, her slight stammer surfacing as it always did when she was upset.

Dan's shoulders slumped. Hurting Amy's feelings always made him feel bad, but honestly, sometimes he couldn't help it. "Look, I know you think it doesn't make sense for us to go to the Bahamas first. But we don't know for sure that the clue is in Jamaica, either."

"True," Amy admitted.

Dan sensed her softening and strained his brain to come up with something that would convince her. "With every clue we've found, it's always been because we discovered a bunch of other stuff along the way, right? In the 'wrong' places. But if we hadn't gone to the wrong places first, we wouldn't have gotten what we needed to find the clue in the *right* place."

His face was a little red now from the effort of trying to explain. "What I mean is, it's turned out that we were *right* to go to the wrong places first. Voilà, the Bahamas!"

Amy burst out laughing. "Do you realize what you're saying? You're admitting that I'm right about Jamaica!"

Dan grinned. "You get to be right, and I get to go to

Oceanus." He punched her on the arm. "That's what's known as win-win."

In their mutual satisfaction, neither of them remembered that the Kabras had a villa in the Bahamas.

The super-rich, super-Lucian family headed by Isabel Kabra, who had already tried to eliminate both Dan and Amy from the hunt.

And who, years before, had murdered their parents.

Nellie rejoined them, bobbing her head in time to whatever was playing on her iPod, as usual. Dan had once suggested that she have the earbuds implanted surgically, since she hardly ever took them out.

"Okay, kids, ticket counter," Nellie said. She nodded approvingly. "Bahamas—now *that's* what I'm talkin' about, dude! Beach chair, here I come!"

On the way to the ticket counter, Nellie stopped in the restroom. When she emerged, she took their passports from them.

They had the routine down pat now: Nellie got in the ticket line and dealt with the agent, while Dan and Amy stood behind her, trying to look as much as possible like two kids traveling with their au pair on a pleasant trip to see nice relatives somewhere. Not like two kids constantly on the run from scheming, murderous, cutthroat relatives, which is what they actually were.

"Three tickets to the Bahamas," Nellie said to the ticket agent.

While he waited, Dan checked his phone messages. He frowned as he listened. "Hamilton called," he said to Amy after he closed the phone.

"What did he want?"

Dan shook his head. "The signal was terrible, he kept cutting in and out. But"—he looked around suspiciously—"somehow his dad already knew where we were going."

Amy gasped. "How is that possible? *We* didn't even know where we were going until, like, five minutes ago! And the only other person—" She stopped, her eyes wide.

"While she was in the bathroom!" Dan exclaimed.

Together they turned and stared at Nellie's back as she stood at the ticket counter.

Amy felt her heart sinking. She squeezed her eyes shut for a moment, remembering other times when Nellie's actions had seemed suspicious. When she opened them again, she saw that Dan looked exactly how she felt. There was distress on every square inch of his face. Even his nose, if that were possible.

In the last few months, they had spent more time with Nellie than anyone else. *She's more than an au pair now—she's like a cousin,* Amy thought. *Maybe even an older sister. How could she possibly—*

"We have to figure out what she's up to," Dan said. "We'll grill her on the plane, where she can't get away from us. But I gotta tell you the rest of what Hamilton said."

After one more worried look at Nellie, Amy turned back toward him.

"So Eisenhower finds out we're going to the Bahamas," Dan said, "and Hamilton didn't really understand it all, but he said his dad said something about a cat, and how we got it all wrong, and the Bahamas wasn't the right place. They're going to South Carolina instead."

"Did he know about the portrait? About Anne Bonny?" Amy asked.

"I don't know. He didn't say anything about her, just something about a cat."

"A cat? Was he talking about Saladin?"

"No. The call kept breaking up, and I didn't really get it all, but definitely not Saladin. Speaking of which—"

He took Saladin out of the pet carrier and stroked the cat for a few moments. Amy could sense that he was still thinking about Nellie and had turned to Saladin for a brief moment of comfort.

Saladin snuggled into Dan's arms and purred—the only one among the three of them who was perfectly content.

CHAPTER 2

Nellie's jaw dropped.

"You're giving *me* the window seat?" she said, incredulous.

She was momentarily stunned by their generosity but didn't hesitate to snatch up this rare gift. She settled into the seat and rested her head against the window.

After takeoff, Dan reached over and plucked the earbuds out of her ears.

"Dude!" she said. "What are you doing?"

"Right question," Dan said. "What are *you* doing?" He pulled the cord out of the iPod and held the earbuds out of her reach.

Amy took the earbuds from Dan and wound the cord neatly, away from Nellie's swiping hand. "Nellie, cut it out," she said. "We—we really need to talk."

Nellie felt a prickle of unease, which she covered with an exasperated sigh. "What's the problem now? You said Europe, I took you to Europe. You said Japan, so I took you there, and then Egypt and Russia and—and I don't even know where else, I can't keep track—and now you said the Bahamas, so we're on our way. What's to talk about?"

Dan crossed his arms sternly. For a fleeting moment, Nellie almost wanted to pat him on the head; with his face so serious, he looked younger somehow.

"How's this for starters," he said. "You somehow magically get us permits to go to Tibet when it takes months for most people. You make one phone call, and all of a sudden we have access to the only helicopter in the world that can get to the top of Everest. The Holts found out that we're going to the Bahamas when no one else but you knew. And in Russia, we heard a message on your phone, asking for a 'status report.'"

Nellie had known this moment would come sooner or later; she'd been praying it would be later.

Well, here goes, she thought. Maybe she could distract them. . . . She tossed her head.

"Great. I leave school to look after you guys; I leave *the country* and go wild-goose-chasing all over the world, which has my parents just thrilled, thank you very much; I even save your necks more than once, and this is the thanks I get?"

Amy looked miserable. Nellie felt a surge of pity. Poor kid. Even with an au pair around, Amy had been shouldering burdens that would crush many adults.

"Nellie, it's not that we don't trust you," she said. "Except that Mr. McIntyre told us not to trust *anyone.* And what Dan said—well, can't you see how it looks kind of fishy to us?"

When the going gets tough, the tough go to the bathroom. Nellie unclasped her seat belt. "If you'll excuse me, I need to use the restroom."

Neither of them budged. "Ah," she said. "So that's why you gave me the window seat. I should have known something was up."

Dan twisted in his seat so he was blocking her way even more.

Nellie bit her lip and stared down at her lap. Thoughts were racing through her head. *That secrecy clause in my contract — fifty thousand dollars extra if I make it through without telling them. Fifty thousand! But I never thought things would get so complicated . . . and it's probably going to get way worse before this is over.*

Without looking up, she could feel their eyes boring into her. They wouldn't be fooled easily.

The truth, then. But not the whole truth. Not who I'm really *working for. Just enough to get them off my back for now.*

She made up her mind. "Okay," she said. "I shouldn't be doing this, but I can't stand it anymore. I'm going to tell you everything."

She pushed the button to recline her seat its full three-quarters of an inch. "Get comfy, kids," she said. "This is a long story."

Amy felt almost like she was falling. It was as if someone had yanked out the rug she was standing on and thrown her completely off balance. Even though she was sitting down.

Nellie, whom they had trusted and relied on and confided in all these weeks . . . she wasn't who they thought she was.

She wasn't a random college student hired by Aunt Beatrice to be their au pair. Not even close.

Nellie had just told them that she was being paid by Mr. McIntyre to look after them—and that all along, she had been sending him reports about their activities.

Without realizing it, Amy took hold of Dan's hand. She looked at him and saw that his face was pale, his lips almost colorless. He didn't pull his hand away.

Nellie was just getting started.

"It was Grace who hired me," she said. "When she made out her will, she must have guessed that you would go after the clues. And that the other teams would have grown-ups or money or both. So she planned it out carefully. She wanted you to have someone along who could help you with all the travel stuff and drive and everything. She told me you'd be hunting for clues and that things might get a little tricky. But she sure as heck didn't tell me what I was really getting into!"

Nellie shook her head.

"I had to interview three different times. For *hours*—man, did she grill me. I knew I had a good shot when I told her that I knew how to fly a plane. And when I finally got the job, she told your Aunt Beatrice that if she fired me, she wouldn't get anything in the will. Your grandmother was one smart lady."

Dan cleared his throat. "No wonder you've lasted so long," he said slowly. "Before you, Aunt Beatrice got rid of au pairs like they were cockroaches or something."

"I *swear* I've never told any of the other teams a single thing," Nellie said. "I tell McIntyre, and he decides what to do with the information. So like with the Bahamas? Yeah, I told him. But I didn't tell the Holts. *He* must have told them, and he must have had his reasons, but he usually doesn't tell me what they are. Otherwise, my only job is to keep you safe."

Silence.

"Don't you get it?" Nellie asked, sounding a little desperate. "Keeping in touch with McIntyre was part of the job description right from the start. It's what they've been paying me for all along."

Finally, Amy forced out a few words. "All this time?" she whispered. "All this time you've been ratting us out for the money?"

"No," Nellie said fiercely. "I got into it because of the money. But now—"

Amy hardly noticed the unfinished sentence because of the hot tears gathering in her eyes. She couldn't have said exactly what she was feeling. Anger? Sadness? Fear? Confusion?

Answer E, all of the above.

How can we believe her now when she's been lying to us for so long?

She unbuckled her seat belt and stood up abruptly. "Excuse us," she said in what she hoped was a cold voice. Still holding Nellie's earbuds, she walked the length of the plane with Dan behind her. When they got to the back, Amy spoke in a ghostly whisper.

"From now on, we don't let her know *anything* about what we're doing," she said.

Dan stared at her in alarm. "We can't do that, Amy! We need her to—I mean, without her—" He was floundering for the right words. "She still has to drive us and—and everything. What are we gonna do about that?"

The stricken expression on his face told her more than his words. What he was really saying was, *We're up against schemers and thieves and murderers! We're just kids—we can't do this on our own!*

She swallowed her own panic and tried to speak calmly. "We'll have to play it by ear. Like, we can tell her where to go but still not say what we're going to do when we get there, see what I mean?"

"Okay," he said after a long pause. "We'll figure it out as we go along, right?"

Amy swiped at her eyes with her sleeve. She still felt shaky, but standing there with Dan had strengthened her resolve a little. *At least we've got each other. . . .*

"Right," she said in as normal a voice as she could manage.

Normal. Amy didn't even know what the word meant anymore.

CHAPTER 3

Traitorous au pair or not, Dan was ready to go.

He was at Oceanus, and nothing was going to stop him from checking out the water park.

"What is it with girls—what's taking so long?"

Dan was in his swim trunks, one hand on the doorknob as he watched Amy and Nellie burrow through their suitcases. Between the three of them, hardly half a dozen words had been spoken since the plane.

Dan had spent the rest of the trip with his thoughts going around in circles. He kept trying to make a mental list of everything that had happened to them when Nellie was around. It wasn't easy, because she'd been around almost the whole time. And no matter how he added things up—from the streets of Paris . . . through the Australian outback . . . to the top of Everest—Nellie had helped them far more than she'd hindered them.

All those hotel rooms . . . Sometimes Nellie had stayed in the same room; other times she'd had her own room. No doubt about it, she would have had plenty of chances to stay in touch with McIntyre and work out a scheme for betrayal. But why take so long? If she was in league with their enemies, why not just get them out of the way as soon as possible?

It just didn't make sense. And Dan had spent enough time on the Clue hunt to know what that meant.

Trouble.

But for the moment, he had decided to put it out of his mind as much as he could.

"C'mon, hurry UP!" he said, jiggling with impatience.

"Sunscreen first," Nellie said, tossing him a tube.

Dan threw his towel on the bed. He smeared a little sunscreen on his arms, stomach, and chest, then rubbed his greasy hands down the front of his legs. "There. Okay?"

"No, not okay," Nellie said. "Your back, your neck, and the backs of your legs, too. And your ears."

"I'll do your back," Amy said quickly.

Dan threw her a glance. It was clear to him that she didn't want Nellie in their lives any more than absolutely necessary—not even doing sunscreen duty.

"I can do it myself," he said, and did an even worse job on his back than he had on his front. Then he grabbed his towel. "I'm not waiting any longer—I'm going without you."

He saw Nellie roll her eyes. "Check in with me at that Dolphin Inlet place at"—she glanced at her watch—"two. And don't lose track of the time. I'm sick of getting freaked out when I can't find you!"

He was out the door before she had finished speaking.

Dan paid for his admission into the water park and got a rubber band to wear on his wrist. First stop: the Sun Palace waterslides. One of the slides looked almost perpendicular! He went down as instructed by the park workers at the top of the slide: legs crossed at the ankles, arms crossed over his chest.

What a breathtaking ride! Literally. Water sprayed into his mouth and got blasted up his nose; by the time he splashed into the pool at the bottom, he was choking and coughing and spitting water. It was glorious.

For two hours, Dan ran around the water park. He couldn't decide if he should first try every single ride once, or if he should do the ones he liked over and over again. This might be his only chance; there wouldn't be any time for fun once they got back on the Clue hunt.

This thought made Dan feel a tiny bit guilty. On the way to the next ride, he spent a few minutes poking around the bushes, looking for a cat. Not just any cat—a calico cat, that was what Hamilton had said.

Then he saw a sign stating that pets weren't allowed in the park. That meant, of course, that the hunt for the cat would have to take place outside the park. How many cats lived in the Bahamas? How were they ever going to find the right one?

But the next ride put any thought of cats out of his mind. He got on an inner tube and went down a steep slide. The slide leveled out and led into a long tunnel. Except it wasn't like the usual waterslide tunnels. This one was made of clear glass—*and it went through a shark tank*. The sharks came really close—if the glass hadn't been there, he could have touched them!

"It was WAY cool," he said to Amy when the threesome met up. He was only seven minutes late.

"Yeah, well, this is way cooler," Nellie said. She held up a string bag full of weird-looking produce.

Amy looked away, and Dan followed her lead in ignoring Nellie.

But Nellie wasn't giving up. "You should have seen all the stuff at the market," she said. "Plantains, jack fruit, custard apples—I bought, like, one of everything!" She pulled out a handful of round dark brown nuts wrapped in what looked like red tentacles.

"Whole nutmegs. The red stuff, that's mace. You can hardly ever find it whole back home—it's way better for cooking than the powdered stuff. Smell." She thrust her hand out at Dan, who immediately backed away.

"No, thanks," he said. "They look like turds. Designer dog turds, like from some fancy miniature show dog."

Nellie put the nutmegs back in her bag. "Why do I even bother trying," she muttered.

"Wait till you hear this," Dan said. "When I was standing in line, some people were talking about how a shark once jumped OUT of the tank and landed on the slide, can you believe it? And then it slid down and ended up in the splash pool!"

Amy shuddered, and Dan knew that she was remembering Australia, where she'd had enough experience with sharks to last a lifetime. "Did anyone get hurt?" she asked anxiously.

Dan shrugged. "Naw. It happened before the park was open for the day." His face fell a little. "But the shark died because of the chlorinated water."

"Poor shark," Nellie said.

"I wish I'd been there!" Dan said. "Just think, I could have gone swimming with a shark!"

Amy made a noise in her throat, fear and loathing combined. "Can we change the subject?" she said. Then she glared at Nellie. "If you'll excuse us—"

Nellie flipped her sunglasses down and shrugged. Amy pulled Dan away a few yards, then held up a brochure.

"Wow. A brochure," Dan said. He mimed a yawn.

"Just listen," she said. "It's the Jolly Codger Pirate's Cove tour. You go on a boat to the smaller islands." She opened the brochure and read aloud from it: "'. . . islands known to have been frequented by famed pirates like Henry Morgan, Blackbeard, and'"—she paused for dramatic effect—"'*Jack Rackham*!'"

"Jack Crackem? Good name for a pirate."

"Rackham," Amy corrected him. "The pirate Anne Bonny joined up with. If we look around the places he's been, maybe we'll find something!"

Dan took the brochure from her and skimmed it.

"Listen to this part," he said. "'Dig for buried treasure! Use of metal detectors and spades included.'" Then his face fell. "Wait, there's this asterisk and it says, 'Coins unearthed on the tour may be redeemed at any resort gift shop.'"

He snorted. "Fake treasure," he said in disgust. "If they want a real challenge, they should try hunting for clues instead."

Amy swallowed a smile. She was pretty sure that not long ago, Dan would have been digging for those coins himself.

They walked back toward Nellie. "We're going on a tour," Amy said. "No need for you to go with us—we'll be back in a couple of hours."

"What kind of tour?" Nellie asked.

"Does it matter?" Amy parried.

"Yes, in fact, it does," Nellie said. "Amy, like it or not, I'm still your au pair. You're my responsibility. That means I get to ask what kind of tour, and you have to answer. If you don't—" She stopped and shrugged.

It was easy to figure out what that shrug meant. It meant *back to Aunt Beatrice.*

Dan whispered into Amy's ear. "Remember what we said? We can tell her where we're going but not what we're doing."

Amy nodded at him, then looked at Nellie. "Okay. We're going on the Jolly Codger boat tour."

"A boat tour," Nellie repeated. "As in, out on the ocean?"

"Um, yeah."

"Then I'm coming with you. And you don't have a choice about that, either."

Amy clenched her fists, struggling to keep her face expressionless. She was forcing herself to act cold and angry so she wouldn't burst into tears. The truth was, ever since Nellie's revelation on the plane, there had been half a dozen times already when Amy had felt like crying.

Nellie wouldn't win any awards at the Au Pair Olympics, if there ever were such a thing. She was careless sometimes, and drove like a maniac, and let them eat too much junk food. But she had always been there for them, and Amy was only now realizing how much she had come to depend on Nellie's presence.

Dan touched her arm. "Come on," he said. They turned away from Nellie and hurried down the path toward the marina.

Nellie followed. They didn't see her turn to glance at a man hidden behind a stand of bougainvillea.

The man nodded at her, and she nodded back.

With a dozen other tourists, the trio boarded a big catamaran called the *Jolly Codger.* As instructed by the crew, they sat around the edges of the tarp that stretched between the two keels. Amy made sure that she and Dan sat several yards away from Nellie.

It was a wonderful day on the water, with a breeze just strong enough to fill the sails and keep the sun from feeling too hot. Amy stared over the edge of the boat. Before, when she had seen photos of the Caribbean Sea, she always thought the pictures must have been retouched, that the water couldn't possibly be such an amazing shade of blue. She was wrong. The water really *was* that incredible.

She thought of the different names for blue colors: azure, turquoise, peacock, cerulean. None of them was quite right—the color of the ocean she was looking at needed its own name, one that hadn't been invented yet. A combination of all those blues.

Azure plus turquoise . . . az-tur-

"Az-tur-pea-lean," she mumbled. She was pleased; it sounded like the name of a fancy color. Maybe if she used it, it would sort of catch on and become a real word someday. "Azturpealean," she repeated.

"Asked her what?" Dan said. "I mean, asked who what?"

Amy reddened. "Never mind."

At that moment, the ship's first mate called out, "Ahoy, everyone!" He was a fit-looking young man wearing cargo shorts and a tank shirt that showed off his perfect biceps. Nellie sat up straighter, and to Amy's amazement, she actually took out the earbuds.

"I'm going to tell you a little about where we're heading today," he said. His accent was singsongy and seemed to fit perfectly with his smile and easy manner. "I hope you're going to have a great time—maybe you're already enjoying yourselves!"

The tourists nodded and smiled.

"Our first stop is coming up soon. It's called Boucan Cay. *Boucan* is an old French word. A *boucan* was a kind of grill used for meat. When European sailors first came to our islands, they would roast their meat on a *boucan*. So the French started calling those sailors '*boucaniers*.'"

"Buccaneers!" Amy said.

"That's right," he said. "In English, we say 'buccaneers'; we've got a very smart young lady there."

The first mate continued his speech. "The Bahamas was a pirate *haven* for a long time. Captain Kidd put in at Exuma Island, not far from here. And maybe the most famous pirate of all—Blackbeard? His real name was Edward Teach. He visited the Bahamas often."

Amy cleared her throat. "Calico Jack Rackham was here, too, wasn't he?"

"Yes, young lady, Jack Rackham, too. Everyone loves the Bahamas!" he joked. "You know the famous skull-and-crossbones flag? Some say it was Jack Rackham who first used it."

Amy poked Dan. "Jack Rackham!" she whispered fiercely.

The catamaran dropped anchor in a beautiful little cove. The crew loaded gear into a motorized rubber raft; everyone else jumped off the boat and swam in to the beach.

Once ashore, most of the kids grabbed metal detectors to hunt for the "buried treasure." Some of the tourists donned snorkeling gear while others, including Nellie, put their towels down on the sand in preparation for some hard work on their tans. Nellie made herself comfortable at once, sunglasses and earbuds firmly in place.

"Young lady!" The first mate waved at Amy. "And you, too, young fella. I have something for you."

"For us?" Amy said. They walked over to where he was working, unloading the raft.

The man reached into one of the pockets of his cargo shorts. "A friend of yours came by before we sailed. He said to give this to you on the island." He handed Amy a folded piece of paper.

"A friend?" Dan echoed. "Did he say his name?"

The mate shook his head. "Sorry."

"What did he look like?"

The mate frowned a little, trying to remember. "He was an older gentleman. Wearing a gray shirt, I think."

"Was he Asian?" Dan asked. Amy knew exactly what he was thinking because she was thinking the same thing: Could it have been Alistair Oh? Or maybe even his uncle Bae?

"I'm afraid I didn't see his face well. He had a hat on and sunglasses, too. Sorry." He smiled. "Will you be wanting snorkel gear?"

"Not right now, thanks," Amy said.

"Actually, yes," Dan contradicted her. He took a mask and snorkel for himself and handed her one, too. "Just in case," he said to her under his breath.

The man gave them a friendly wave. "You tell your friend"—he gestured toward Nellie—"to move her towel if she doesn't want to get wet. The tide will be coming in soon."

Amy and Dan headed away from the other tourists to one side of the cove where there were rocks to sit on. With Dan looking over her shoulder, Amy unfolded the piece of paper.

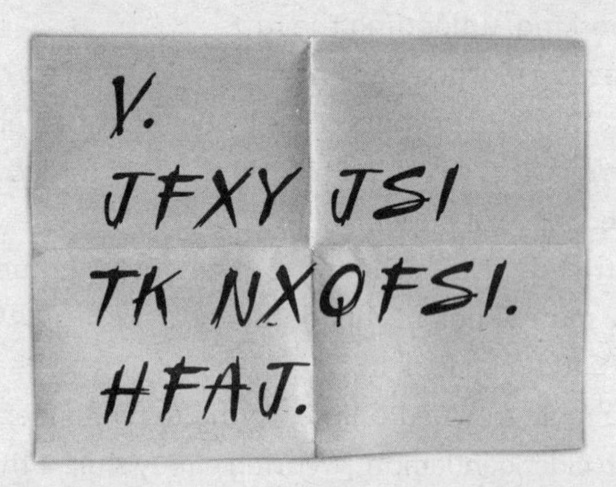

"Code," Dan groaned. "Why does it always have to be so hard? Why can't we just get what we need straight up for once?"

Amy sighed, too. "We don't even know if it's good or bad." Mysterious hints like this one had surfaced before. Some had been helpful, but others had led them straight into traps.

"Either way we still have to figure it out," Dan said.

"Let's get started," Amy said. "First letter, V. V for *victory*? What other words start with V—*vegetable, valentine*—"

"Right. Someone's sending us a valentine in the middle of fall. Someone who wants us to be victorious. And eat more vegetables."

"Very funny," she said. "At least I'm trying."

"We'll never get it that way," Dan said. "Not by guessing—it's way too random. There has to be some kind of pattern."

Amy looked sheepish. "You're right. Sorry, I was being stupid."

Dan raised his eyebrows, surprised by her apology. "Okay, let me think a minute." He stared at the paper for a few moments, then spoke again.

"What if every letter stands for a different letter, like the code we had in South Africa?"

Amy's face lit up. "Yeah. See the V all by itself? It has to stand for either I or A—those are the only two words in English that have just one letter."

"It's probably not even English," Dan moaned. "It's probably from some language that has *hundreds* of one-letter words."

Amy shook her head. "Chances are it's in English. Somebody wanted us to have it, and it wouldn't make sense if we couldn't figure it out."

"Okay, but look. The V has a period after it. 'I,

period.' Or 'A, period.' Neither one makes sense."

Amy sighed. "So we're back to guessing again?"

"No, wait. What if the V isn't a letter? What if—" Dan paused. His eyes began to gleam. "What if it's a *number?*"

"A number?" Amy echoed. She furrowed her brow. Dan was almost twitching with excitement now, but he let her have a moment to figure it out.

"OH!" she exclaimed. "Roman numerals—it's the number five!"

Dan hopped down off the rock. He found a stick of driftwood and began writing in the damp sand.

"Five," he said as he worked, "that's the key."

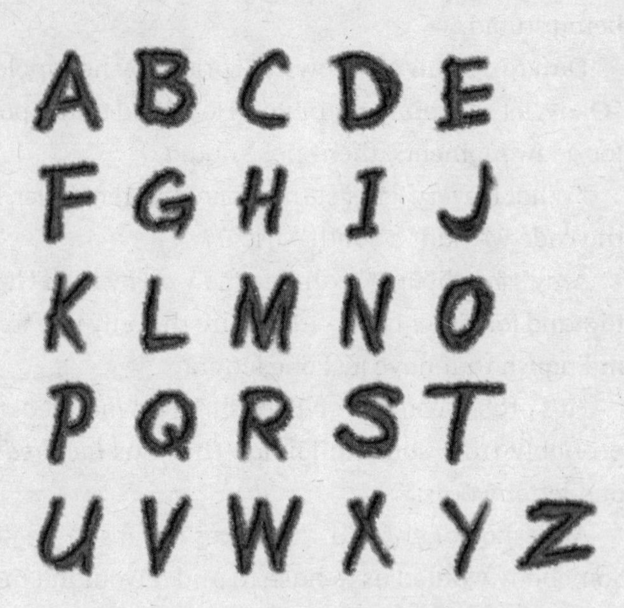

"Now we take each letter and count five, and that should do it! What's the first word?"

Amy read aloud. "J – F – X – Y."

"Wait, not so fast. J—that's an O . . ." Dan wrote again on the sand. "O . . . then F equals K . . . X, C . . . Y, D." He stared at the letters. "OKCD? That's not a word." He scuffed his feet in disgust and kicked the sand to obliterate what he had just written. "I was so sure I'd figured it out."

Meanwhile, Amy was still sitting on the rock. Dan had written the alphabet while facing her, so she was seeing it upside down.

"Hang on a second." She glanced back and forth between the paper in her hand and the alphabet on the sand, sometimes tilting her head to read the upside-down letters.

Then she looked up at him.

"You did figure it out," she said.

"Huh?" He stopped with his foot in mid-stamp.

"Just go the other way," she said. "Count backwards." She hopped down off the rock to join him, reading what was on the paper while he counted out the corresponding letters and wrote them in the sand.

It didn't take long. They stared at the completed message.

"Oh, no," Amy said—at the same time that Dan said, "Cool!"

CHAPTER 4

Natalie Kabra had been having nightmares for more than a week.

The same dream every night, in perfect clarity and detail: Amy Cahill—her hair looking like it had never been styled in her entire life—and her brother, Dan, (ditto) in an airplane hangar, tied to chairs, helpless as the propeller of a plane came closer and closer.

But there was no noise.

Their mouths were wide open, screaming, and the propeller was whirling at top speed. Yet the silence was complete, as if someone had hit the MUTE button on a TV remote.

In the dream, Natalie was standing right next to them. She wasn't tied to a chair, but she couldn't move, either; she was frozen where she stood. She could see Ian beside her mother, his face ashen with dread. The propeller would hit Dan first, then Amy, and then—

The volume came back on again, full blast.

But still no propeller noise, no screaming. Just one sound.

Laughter.

That sound always jerked Natalie out of sleep. Instantly, she was heart-thumpingly, sweat-drenchingly awake. She would turn on her bedside lamp immediately. She had to reassure herself that she was in her own room, every inch of it designed by the same decorator who worked for the British royal family. The familiar paintings on the walls (originals, of course), her custom-made desk and chair in their usual positions, her perfect couture outfit for the next day hanging on the closet door. Despite these reassurances, it always took her a long time to fall asleep again.

And every morning, the dream seemed foolish, as bad dreams so often do. The horror faded, and Natalie imagined that she had remembered it wrong, that she wasn't standing next to Dan and Amy but in her proper place, alongside her mother and brother.

Yes. She was, after all, a Kabra. The very best kind of Cahill. None of the others even came close, most especially Dan and Amy.

The thought would have been laughable if it weren't so pathetic.

EAST END OF ISLAND.

CAVE.

Amy and Dan stared at the decoded message scrawled in the sand.

"Not again," Amy said in alarm.

Dan snapped his fingers. "Maybe there are cats living in the cave!"

"Well, if there are, I bet they aren't nice fuzzy house pets," Amy pointed out. "Tigers and—and panthers, those are the kinds of cats that live in caves."

"Tigers don't live in the Caribbean," Dan said. "And stray cats might live in caves."

Amy glanced around quickly. "Stamp it out," she said. Dan complied, and the water did its part by washing away some of the letters.

They walked back to where Nellie was sunbathing to pick up their backpacks.

"Where are you going?" she asked, raising herself on one elbow.

"To a c—" Dan started to say.

"For a walk," Amy said loudly, cutting him off.

"I'll go with you," Nellie said, sitting up.

"No, thanks," Amy said.

Nellie pushed her sunglasses onto the top of her head. "Amy, come on," she said. "Whatever you might think of me now, you gotta give me one thing: I've always done my best to keep you guys safe."

Amy hesitated. Caves could be dangerous. If anything happened . . .

Potential danger or potential traitor, which was worse? Once again, the hunt was forcing Amy to make choices she had never dreamed she'd face.

"You can come with us," she said to Nellie. "We're

going to a cave. But once we get there, we go in by ourselves, got it?"

That way, if they found something there, they could keep it a secret from Nellie.

Nellie looked hurt for just a moment, then lowered her sunglasses. "Got it," she said in a neutral voice.

They began walking east. As they passed the first mate, Nellie asked if she could borrow a coil of rope.

"No problem," the mate said. "What do you need it for?"

"Uh, we thought we'd play tug-of-war," Dan said.

The man laughed and handed Nellie the rope. She slung it over her shoulder.

"Cave. Rope. Good idea," Amy muttered, not quite loud enough for Nellie to hear.

The island was a tiny one; it took them only about ten minutes to reach the eastern end. They left the curve of golden sand behind and walked along rocky outcrops that jutted into the sea. *The azturpealean sea,* Amy thought. *Very poetic.*

"The rocks end, so the cave must be around there somewhere," Dan said, pointing to the area in front of them. They walked back and forth for a while but found nothing that looked like a cave entrance.

"We'll have to wade," Dan said. "The entrance must face the ocean." He pulled off his T-shirt and dropped it and his backpack on the sand. He took a flashlight out of the pack; experience had taught both Cahills that a flashlight often came in handy while Clue hunting. Then he picked his way through the rocks and sat down on the edge of one. After donning the mask and snorkel, he splashed into the water.

Amy and Nellie followed more cautiously. The water was only hip deep and as warm as a nice bath, but there were rocks protruding from the sandy bottom. Their sole purpose in life seemed to be to cause sprained ankles.

"Here!" Dan called out.

He was standing in front of a group of larger rock formations that blocked their view of the beach they had seen earlier. The cave was in a natural depression. From the shore, the rocks looked no taller than Dan, but the seabed sloped lower here. The rocks were taller than Nellie, and the water was up to Dan's waist.

The girls joined him. The cave opening was a little wider than one person but not quite wide enough for two, and just high enough so that Nellie could have entered without ducking. Dan picked up a stone from the seabed and threw it into the opening.

It made only a splashing sound, which meant that it hadn't hit a wall.

"It goes in pretty far," he said.

"Ta-da," Nellie said, taking the coil of rope off her shoulder and holding it up.

They tied themselves together: one end of the rope around Dan's waist, a couple of yards of slack between him and Amy, and Nellie holding the coil.

"If you're not back in fifteen minutes, I'm coming in after you," Nellie said.

Dan was already inside the cave. "Here, kitty kitty kitty," he called. "Meow? Anybody home?"

"Wait," Amy said. She turned back toward Nellie. "We'll pull twice if—if we need you to come in before that," she said.

Nellie nodded. She leaned against a rock a few feet away from the entrance and got busy tying the rope around her waist.

Amy took a few steps through the water, then paused again. One more step and she'd be in the full gloom of the cave. She looked around carefully. Once, when they were in a tomb, they had missed an important hint that was right on the stairs as they entered. She didn't want to make the same mistake again.

"Dan!" she said, her voice quiet but urgent.

She was looking at the wall right above the cave entrance.

At a crude carving of a bear—the top half, its head and front paws, with their vicious claws.

The symbol of the Tomas clan.

Nellie made sure the rope around her waist had a good solid knot in it. Things looked peaceful enough, but with those two, it never seemed to stay that way for long. . . . She held the rest of the coil in her hand and watched as it slowly payed out. Before it had reached its full length, the rope stopped moving. That meant Dan and Amy had stopped moving, too. Good—maybe they would come out again soon.

She looked longingly at her backpack, which she had set down on the beach before entering the water. Her iPod was in there. No music in her ears, but there was always music in her head. She leaned against the rock behind her and started humming.

"Miss Gomez."

Nellie almost fell over into the water. She caught herself just in time and planted her feet as firmly as she could in the shifting sand.

She would know that voice anywhere. Soft, raspy, as if it hardly ever got any use . . . Her heart pounding, she looked to her right, and there, standing on the rocks between her and the shore, was the man in black.

Except that now, he was the man in gray. He was wearing a gray long-sleeved camp shirt, gray trousers, and a gray bucket hat pulled down over his brow. Even his sunglasses were gray.

Nellie squared her shoulders, faced him straight on, and lifted her chin defiantly.

"Dude," she said. "I wish, just once, you wouldn't sneak up on me like that."

The man in black—now the man in gray—glanced into the mouth of the cave. "Not so loud," he rasped.

Nellie shrugged. She was always nervous when he was around, and now she tried to cover it with nonchalance. "I'll be able to tell when they're on their way back," she said. "The rope will move."

She looked him up and down. "I hear gray is very fashionable this year."

"My customary attire would have stood out too much in this environment," he said. "But that is of little consequence. Your message said you have news?"

"Yeah," she said. "I had to tell them about working for McIntyre."

He was silent for a moment. "That is unfortunate," he said at last.

The chill in his voice made her neck prickle. *Don't let him know he's getting to you,* she thought.

"Easy for you to say," she said. "You get to skulk around and stay hidden and never talk to them. I have to *live* with them! You have no idea how hard it is—"

He held up his hand. "Your efforts have been appreciated."

She sniffed. "Well, they don't trust me now. But it'll make some things easier. They won't get all suspicious if they catch me communicating with McIntyre now. And I didn't say anything about *you* or—or anything else. So technically the terms of my contract are still intact."

She was pleased with how that last line came out; she had been rehearsing it in her head.

"Agreed," he said. "I trust there will be no further

breaches. It also appears that they deciphered the most recent message. Did you help them?"

"No way," she said. "I told you, they don't trust me. Especially Amy. They didn't even tell me about it."

He leaned toward her and lowered his voice even more. "I am sure that I don't need to remind you how crucial these next few days will be. The Madrigals are most anxious to make their final move."

Nellie almost choked on the wave of guilt that rose in her. *How can I do this to those kids?*

You have to, another part of her answered. *You can't quit now. It's not just about the money and you know it.*

"Can't you give them a little more time?" she pleaded. "They're only kids!"

He shook his head. "There is too much at stake."

Nellie shivered and felt a creeping sensation up her spine. Then she realized it wasn't just the conversation that was making her feel that way. The tide had risen while they were talking, and the water was now up to her waist. She looked at the cave entrance. There was less than a yard of clearance above the water now.

"They can't stay in there much longer," she said. She cursed, realizing that while two tugs on the rope meant she should go *into* the cave, they hadn't set up a signal meaning they should come *out* of it.

"I better check—" Nellie turned to look at the man in gray again.

He was gone.

CHAPTER 5

It wasn't *quite* pitch-black in the cave. A lighter shade of black, if that was possible.

Dan was leading the way. The light from the entrance and the beam of the flashlight showed that the walls and ceiling were pitted and craggy. Dan stopped every step or two so he could shine the flashlight's beam all around.

It was slow going. After about twenty cautious paces, Dan reached the far wall.

"That's it," he said. "It doesn't go any farther."

They now knew that the cave was not very big, perhaps fifteen feet across and thirty feet long, narrower at the entrance and toward the ceiling. No passages branched off, nor were there any niches or alcoves in the rock walls.

"We must have missed something," Amy said.

"How do you know we're in the right place? There could be another cave around here somewhere."

"With the Tomas crest over the door?"

"Well, no cats in here, that's for sure," he said.

"Let's walk around the edge now," Amy suggested.

They turned to their right and made their way slowly around the side of the cave.

Dan touched the wall gingerly. It was rough, maybe granite. The water slapped at the walls all around, not big waves, just wavelets. Each small surge brought the water to almost chest level.

Chest level?

"The tide!" he said. "It's coming in!"

"Then we better find it quick," Amy said grimly.

They took another couple of steps to the right. Dan flashed the light at the side wall.

"Not so fast," Amy said. "Do it, like, a square foot at a time."

They went over that section of wall slowly. Dan glanced anxiously down at the water. Then it hit him. They were only searching above the waterline!

"Oh, no," he said. "What if it's down there somewhere?" He pointed the flashlight beam through the water.

Amy groaned. "We'll have to come back when the tide is out all the way. Maybe we could just sort of guard the place until the tide goes down—Nellie could go back to the boat and tell them we're staying here—"

Dan hardly heard her. "Here," he said, handing her the flashlight. "Aim it straight down there." He pointed the beam of light at where the wall of the cave joined the ocean floor. It wasn't a neat, right-angle seam as it would have been for a room indoors; there were rocks of all sizes sticking out from both the ocean floor and the wall itself.

He hadn't really *seen* anything. It was so dark, with the water moving and the flashlight beam wavering. . . . But maybe he *had* seen something, just not clearly enough or long enough for his brain to put a name to it.

He adjusted his mask and snorkel, took a deep breath, and ducked under the surface. Bent over, half swimming and half crawling, he groped around the rocks at the bottom, trying to remember what he had seen or thought he'd seen. Here? Or closer to the wall?

He surfaced and spat out the snorkel mouthpiece. "Can't you hold the light steady?" he said. "It's wobbling around so much I can't get a bead on anything."

"I *am* holding it still," she said. "It's the waves. And the reflection."

"Refraction," he corrected her.

"Whatever. Dan, it's not going to be safe here much longer." The water level now rose to Amy's chest, which meant that it was almost up to Dan's neck.

He knew she was right. "I'm gonna go down once or twice more," he said. "I think—"

But he didn't finish the thought. Maybe that would jinx him. He fixed the snorkel in place again and went back underwater.

Rock. Bigger rock. Rock. He touched each one with

his fingertips as he moved toward the wall to make sure he wasn't missing anything. Rock, tiny pebbles, rock . . .

Wait. Tiny pebbles? There weren't any other tiny pebbles around. All the rocks were at least the size of baseballs. Those pebbles . . .

He surfaced. "Gimme the flashlight," he said, trying to keep his voice calm.

"Did you find something?"

"No. I don't know." He shone the light on the area he'd been searching. "Man! Why didn't we bring an underwater flashlight?"

One more circuit with the light, a square foot at a time . . .

"There! Hold the light right here—don't move a muscle!"

He went back under again. They weren't tiny pebbles. They were links that formed some kind of chain lodged firmly between two rocks. He got two fingers under the links and tugged. They didn't budge.

Dan put his foot on the chain and stood up straight again. When his head broke the surface, it was the only body part that did. The water was up to his chin now, and the waves grew rougher as the water was forced into the narrower confines of the cave's upper reaches.

"Dan! We have to get out of here!" Amy was now holding the flashlight up above her shoulder to keep it out of the water.

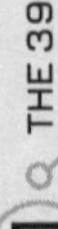

"I've got something! It's right here!"

He went back down again and yanked frantically at the chain. With his other hand, he pushed at one of the rocks. It didn't budge, either. He switched to using both hands on the rock . . . was it moving?

Just then he felt a hand on his shoulder, yanking him up. "Dan, come on!"

"No!" he said, and inhaled a little seawater as a wave rose over the top of the snorkel. He hacked and coughed for a few moments, feeling his chest start to tighten.

"Just one more try," he gasped, and plunged back down again.

With all his might, Dan shoved at the rock. Finally, he felt it give, grabbed the chain, and gave it a yank. It came free!

He stood up straight again and wrapped the chain around his wrist twice. Only the tips of his toes were touching the bottom now, and the snorkel was useless — the waves kept swamping it. The air space in the cave had shrunk to only a couple of feet.

Amy hadn't said a word, and Dan knew what that meant. She was frozen in panic.

"We gotta swim," he said. "Come on, it's not far —"

Amy dropped the flashlight. It stayed lit until it hit the bottom, then blinked out.

"DAN! AMY!" It was Nellie, hollering from the cave entrance. "You gotta get out of there! I'm going to start pulling on the rope! On the count of three—one, two, THREE!"

Ahead of him, Dan saw Amy suddenly shoot forward and up; she must have launched herself off the bottom at the same instant that Nellie pulled. Amy crashed head first into the jagged rock ceiling. She reeled backward, knocking him over.

When they both came up again, he saw her face in the dim light from the entrance. There were dark streams running down from her forehead.

Blood.

Lots of it.

"STOP!" Dan yelled. "Nellie, stop pulling!"

"What's wrong?" she yelled back.

"It's Amy! She hit her head—" He gurgled as a wave washed over him.

Amy was staggering around, clearly disoriented.

"Amy!" Dan grabbed the rope and started pulling her toward him. She fought against the pull of the rope around her waist.

Dan pushed off the bottom and got his head above water long enough to take half a breath. He swam to Amy and tried to grab her arm. She slipped out of his grasp and began stumbling in the wrong direction, back into the cave. He caught her again and yanked her toward him as hard as he could.

"AMY!" he yelled. "THIS WAY!"

Amy gurgled and coughed; she must have swallowed some water. But at least she wasn't fighting against him now. He put one arm under her shoulders and began paddling with the other. His feet made motions between kicking and bicycling as he tried to move forward.

He had never been so scared. Where had all that blood come from? He tried to yell for Nellie but could manage only a strangled "Nel—" before a wave swamped him.

He struggled to keep Amy's head above water. His own lungs were bursting. He wrestled both their heads up and took a breath that was more water than air. Choking, he felt his grip on Amy start to loosen, and he tried frantically to tighten his arm around her.

Nellie must have found the muscle power of three grown men because suddenly, Dan and Amy were pulled almost straight into her with one last great heave.

But they weren't out of the cave yet. Nellie had been standing a few yards inside the entrance, or maybe their weight had pulled her in. Her head was still above water—barely.

Now she grabbed Amy under the arms. "GO!" she yelled.

Dan felt his arm squeeze his sister even tighter. He couldn't seem to let go of her. For a terrible moment, it was almost as if he and Nellie were fighting over Amy.

"DAN! I've got her! Now GET OUT OF HERE!"

Dan flailed out of the cave on the backwash of the next wave.

It was a different world.

Outside the cave, the sun was shining and the waves were gentle. A beautiful day at the beach. Dan stumbled, his legs feeling as soggy as his brain. As he righted himself, Nellie came out of the cave sideways, pulling Amy with her.

They half dragged, half carried Amy up to the beach. Nellie turned her on her side in the warm sand and bent over her.

"She's breathing," Nellie said, and the relief on her face was unmistakable.

Dan dropped to his knees on Amy's other side, behind her. Then Amy made a dreadful coughing, hacking noise.

Dan thought it was the nicest sound he had ever heard.

Amy tried to say something and coughed some more. Nellie pounded her on the back, and Amy finally got her breath.

"Dan," she croaked. "Is Dan okay?"

The lump that rose in Dan's throat made *him* start coughing. Now they were both coughing and hacking, and Dan was laughing and maybe crying a little, too, or maybe there was still seawater in his eyes.

Nellie shook her head. "What's so funny? You both nearly drowned!"

Amy rolled onto her back and looked at Dan.

"Yuck," he said, and gave her a feeble smile. "You look terrible."

Back on the catamaran, Nellie wouldn't let the first mate anywhere near Amy.

"But I am trained in first aid," he said.

"So am I," she retorted. "Red Cross certified—can you top that?"

The mate handed her the first-aid kit.

Once the blood was cleaned off Amy's face, Dan was relieved to see that she looked a whole lot better. Except for the three-inch gash on her forehead just above her left temple.

"Head wounds bleed a lot, so they usually look worse than they are," Nellie said, all business now. She cleaned the cut and used suture tape to close it. Then she put a gauze dressing on it. She moved her finger in front of Amy's face to make sure her eyes were tracking it and had Amy answer some simple math questions.

"We'll get you checked out by a doctor as soon as we get back to the hotel," Nellie said. "For now, you rest." Dan helped her arrange some deck pillows and towels into a makeshift bed on the catamaran's tarp.

Amy kept insisting that she was fine, and that she didn't want to spoil the rest of the tour for the other passengers. But the captain was firm. The boat would return to Oceanus and drop off Nellie and her charges so Amy could see a doctor.

Nellie went with the first mate to get Amy something to drink. Dan sat down next to Amy. His legs still felt shaky, and his stomach was tight with nerves. It was strange—they'd been in and out of danger a whole bunch of times before, but he couldn't remember ever being that scared. When he'd seen the blood all over Amy's face . . . He shivered in spite of the sunshine.

If Nellie can't be trusted, and if—if something worse had happened to Amy . . .

He swallowed hard, not daring to finish the thought.

Dan gazed solemnly at the sea. There were lots of boats out today—a racing sloop with tall white sails, a dinghy with a rainbow-striped spinnaker, a fancy black yacht. . . . He stretched one arm out along the railing and felt something scratch his wrist.

"Hey!" he said, pulling up his sleeve, "I forgot about this!"

It was the chain around his wrist, which had been covered up by his sleeve.

"What is it?" Amy asked eagerly.

Dan turned so that his back was to the rest of the boat. He took the chain off his wrist. Something dangled from it—a slender, curved, pointy object a couple of inches long. Both the chain and the object were mostly a dull gray now, but it was easy to see that they had once been yellow.

"Gold," Dan said, very pleased. "Silver might have been okay, too, but anything else would have gotten ruined by the saltwater."

"A shark tooth?" Amy said. She touched it hesitantly, as if she were afraid it might bite her.

Dan shook his head. "No, those are a lot more triangle shaped," he said, "and flatter. This looks more like some kind of—of claw. Or talon, maybe."

"Wow," Amy said. "That would be one big bird."

"An eagle or a hawk could have a talon this big."

"Or a superchicken." Amy giggled.

Dan looked at her. It wasn't like Amy to make jokes when it came to the hunt for Clues. Maybe that knock on the head *had* done her some real harm.

As if he had spoken aloud, she said, "My brain must be mush. It's so simple."

"Your brain? Your brain is simple?"

"Very funny. It all makes sense. Tomas cave, right?"

Dan felt as if a lightbulb had switched on in his brain. Amy was so darn smart.

"Bear claw," they said at the same time.

CHAPTER 6

Ian adjusted the focus on the binoculars.

"He's definitely got something in his hand," he said, "but I'm not sure what it is. It could be—it's long and pointed—"

"Another fang?" Natalie asked.

She glanced at her mother's wrist. Isabel was wearing a bracelet of heavy gold links that held a small collection of intricate charms. *So classy,* Natalie thought. *Why do the masses persist in thinking that more is always better?*

One of the charms was a gold wolf fang. Natalie didn't know why the charm was important, only that it was somehow part of the Clue hunt, and that Isabel was sure there were other charms like it out there somewhere.

They were on the Kabra family yacht, the *Universal Force.* Natalie loved everything about the sleek black boat, especially its name. It had been Isabel's inspiration, but Natalie and Ian had done the legwork. With the help of the Internet, they had researched anagram sites and found the perfect name.

Universal Force was an anagram for *Lucians Forever.*

"Whatever it is, they've found it," Isabel said in a grim voice. She lowered the binoculars and stared at Ian, her eyes like laser beams. "How long have we known that the cave was a Tomas site? And you searched it how many times?"

Ian muttered something under his breath. Natalie glanced nervously between her mother and her brother. "Maybe it wasn't there before. Maybe it got washed in by the waves." she said. "Or somebody put it there, um, just now."

She cringed from the force of Isabel's withering glare. "Don't you dare make excuses for him, Natalie," Isabel said. "Those brats have bested you *again.*"

Isabel shoved the throttle. The boat leaped forward.

"I'm telling you both," she said, "I won't stand for it anymore!"

Natalie knew that to the rest of the world, she and Ian were golden. They had it all: money, good looks, intelligence. It was only around Isabel that Natalie found herself feeling uncertain, hesitant, afraid to make a mistake.

Especially lately. It wasn't easy having a mother who was always perfectly dressed and exquisitely coiffed and strode through the world as if she owned it. (She did, in fact, own considerable chunks of it.)

Natalie stood alone at the *Force*'s bow, trying to collect herself. Her mother was always at her worst when it came to Dan and Amy. They made her so angry! Why did they have to keep fouling things up for Natalie's family?

The Kabras had to win the race for the Clues, it was as simple as that. Who else could possibly handle the power and responsibility? The dunderheaded Holts? The shallow, media-crazed Wizards? The inept Alistair Oh and his decrepit uncle?

Any one of them as head of the Cahill clan would be a complete disaster.

From the beginning of the Clue hunt, Ian and Natalie had worked to find the answers, sometimes even competing against each other in an effort to win Isabel's approval. But time after time, Dan and Amy had defeated them.

How was it possible? *They're nothing! No family, no power, not even any staff—except for that crazy au pair—how could they have beaten us so many times?*

And the worst of it was that her mother had lost faith in Natalie. In Ian, too. Since their failure in Russia, Isabel had taken over, and nothing Natalie or her brother did was ever right.

Now Natalie shivered in the full sunshine. The scene in the hangar was haunting her waking hours as well as her dreams. The propeller, rotating slowly at first, then faster, faster, until it was a lethal blur . . . the boy tied to the chair being pushed closer and closer . . .

Natalie squeezed her eyes shut tight, which did nothing to block out the image in her mind.

She wouldn't have done it.

She'd have stopped the propeller somehow. At the very last second.

She wouldn't really have killed them. Not like that.

Natalie herself, along with Ian, had tried several times to thwart Dan and Amy in ways that were . . . less than pleasant. But their ruses were all planned so they would never have to witness the end results. Which meant that Natalie could—and did—choose not to consider the grisly consequences of their actions. She focused instead on the hope that Dan and Amy would be out of the way once and for all.

When Isabel stepped in, some of her plans had followed a similar pattern: the poisonous snakes in the mine, the fire in Indonesia. If those schemes had worked, the Kabras wouldn't have been there when the Cahills actually met their doom. The sharks in Australia—that would have been different, but Natalie hadn't been there. So she had conveniently been able to put any thought of bloodshed out of her mind.

Until the propeller had started its deathly whirl.

Overhead, a seagull made a harsh sound, almost like it was laughing . . . like the laughter in her dream.

Natalie gasped and opened her eyes. The person laughing in her dream was Isabel!

Could her mother be so cruel and heartless that she would *laugh* at the prospect of a violent and agonizing death for the Cahills? Is that what the dream meant?

No!

She's perfect! Or as perfect as anyone can be. And nobody really understands her except me—not even Ian. She might be a bit demanding at times, but that's only because she's so determined. She's warned me about this—that people always resent when a woman has a lot of power. . . .

Natalie knew that Ian was having doubts about their mother. She had seen it in small ways: how he wouldn't quite meet their mother's eyes and often muttered under his breath when she was around. Perhaps it wasn't surprising; after all, he was the one who had turned on the propeller, following Isabel's orders.

But what else could that laugh possibly mean?

Natalie searched her mind desperately. *It could mean—I don't know—there has to be some other explanation—*

Suddenly, she lifted her head and laughed herself.

It was all a joke! She just wanted to scare them! That's what my dream is trying to tell me—that laugh—she was joking; she never would have gone through with it!

Practically floating with relief, Natalie made her way down the stairs to her cabin. The things in her shipboard closet from the last fashion season simply had to be thrown away.

"Ish ish AY!"

It was not easy to speak clearly through a gargantuan mouthful of cheeseburger. Dan was trying to say "This is GREAT!" but the words came out filtered through ground sirloin and two slices of cheese.

Nellie had organized everything. The resort's doctor was waiting for them at the hotel. She examined Amy and diagnosed a laceration, a contusion, and a possible slight concussion. After redressing the wound, the doctor told Amy to take it easy for the rest of the day.

Nellie had called room service, too; there were burgers and shakes ready for them when they got back to the room. Once again, Dan didn't know what to think. If Nellie was trying to help their enemies, she was certainly going about it backwards.

Now a taxi was out front to take them to the airport. The Cahills had decided that it was time to visit Jamaica.

After they ate, Dan dragged the luggage and

Saladin's carrier to the taxi while Nellie checked out. As the driver opened the trunk, Dan got an eerie feeling in the back of his neck as if someone were watching him. He turned slowly and looked around.

At the side of the hotel's big sweeping forecourt, there were bougainvillea bushes in full bloom. Crazy colors—pink and red and sort of orangey. Pretty, if you liked that sort of thing.

Dan stared at the bushes.

Nobody there. He was just about to turn back when he saw it: a pair of eyes peering at him through the branches at the base of one of the bushes.

Green eyes.

Green *cat* eyes.

He dropped his backpack and took off running.

"Hey!" Amy said. "What are you doing?"

"Cat," he yelled back over his shoulder.

"Dan, wait!"

No use. Dan was chasing the cat, which had bolted as soon as he made a move toward it.

The cat led Dan away from the hotel, down the long driveway to a parade of small shops. He lost sight of it when it darted around to the back.

Panting, Dan trotted after it. The buildings were all nice wooden houses, painted in bright tropical colors, with front porches, chairs, windchimes. . . . Everything at the front was very tourist-tidy.

But around the back, there were dumpsters and garbage cans. Cat territory.

By the time Dan got back to the hotel twenty minutes later, Amy was frantic and Nellie was furious. In fact, he heard them before he saw them.

"You can't go running off like that!"

"Where have you been?"

"I tried to—"

"What were you doing?"

"I was just—"

"What were you thinking?"

"I thought maybe—"

Nellie put two fingers in her mouth and gave a shrill whistle. "Time out!" she yelled. "You can tell us all about it in the car."

She hustled them into the backseat and tossed Dan's backpack onto his lap.

"OW!" he yelped. He was wearing shorts, and the pack had landed partly on his bare legs.

"I now know the true meaning of pain," he said sadly. "Cat scratches on top of sunburn."

"But it wasn't just any cat," Dan said. He was trying to explain the reason for his sudden disappearance. "It was a *calico* cat. I tried to catch it, but it scratched the heck out of me and got away."

He rubbed at one of the scratches. "I don't think we should leave here yet," he said. "We still haven't figured out this cat thing, and Hamilton *said*—"

"Why in the world would—oh." Amy was quiet for a moment. Then she started to laugh.

"What's so funny?" Dan demanded.

She didn't answer, or rather, she couldn't answer. She was laughing too hard. Dan looked at her for a few moments, first puzzled, then annoyed.

"Amy!" he said impatiently. It was no fun watching someone laugh at you.

Finally, Amy gasped for breath and wiped her eyes. "Jack Rackham," she said. "The pirate. He did some pirating here, and later Anne Bonny joined up with him, right?"

"So what?"

"He—his name—" Amy started laughing again, but Dan glared at her so fiercely that she got herself under control more quickly this time.

"His nickname"—snort, chortle—"was *Calico Jack.*"

"Calico Jack?"

Amy's laughing jag released a few final giggles. "Hamilton must have been saying 'Calico Jack,' but you thought he said 'calico cat.'"

"I get it, you don't have to spell it out for me." Dan's face was already pink from sunburn and running in the heat, but he felt it getting even pinker.

Time to change the subject. "Nellie, do you have any first-aid cream handy?"

As they drove away, none of them noticed the black SUV pulling into traffic behind them.

Or, for that matter, the discreet gray sedan following them both.

At the Montego Bay airport in Jamaica, Nellie rented a car, then found a hotel. It was only about eight o'clock in the evening, local time, but they were all exhausted. Dan fell asleep in his clothes.

After breakfast the next morning, they headed for the car on Amy's instructions.

"Kingston," she said.

"Huh," Nellie snorted. Her hand was on the key in the ignition slot, but she wasn't starting the engine. "How about something like, 'Nellie, dear, would you please be so good as to take us to Kingston?' Then I could say, 'Why, yes, Amy, I'd be totally down with that. It's beyond cool to work with such awesome kids.'"

Amy caught herself just before she giggled. She had almost forgotten about keeping Nellie at arm's length. *Probably a subconscious thing,* she thought, *me wanting everything to be all right again . . .*

"We're in a hurry," she said tersely.

"When are we *not* in a hurry," Nellie grumbled.

It was a long drive from Montego Bay to Kingston; the hotel desk clerk had told them it would probably take almost four hours.

Amy needed to talk to Dan, but not in front of Nellie. The solution was simple enough.

"Put your earbuds in," she said, "and turn the music up loud."

Nellie sighed but did as ordered. Then Amy climbed into the backseat. She saw Nellie's eyes flick to the rear-view mirror, so she put her hand over her mouth as she spoke to Dan in a low voice. Nellie probably couldn't lip-read, but Amy wasn't taking any chances.

"I've been reading this really interesting book," she said. *"A General History of the Pyrates*—pyrates spelled with a 'y,' the old-fashioned way."

"Amy—"

"Put your hand over your mouth."

Dan complied after a quick glance at the back of Nellie's head. "We were in the Bahamas for about eight hours. You spent more than half that time on a boat and the other half in a doctor's office. *When* did you have time to buy a book?"

"I didn't buy it. I downloaded it in the Oceanus library. While you were at the water park. And I read it on the plane just now."

"The whole thing?"

"No, silly. Just the chapters about Anne Bonny and Jack Rackham. Anyway, the book was written by this guy named Captain Charles Johnson. But a lot of people think that was a pseudonym and that it was really written by Daniel Defoe—you know, the guy who wrote *Robinson Crusoe*."

"Oh, yeah," he said. "I knew that. But not everybody has a library catalog for a brain like you do."

Amy ignored his last comment. She went on. "Anne Bonny joined Rackham's crew. She dressed up as a man and learned how to sail and sword fight and everything, and nobody on the ship except Calico Jack knew she was a woman."

"Pretty cool," Dan said.

"They had a baby in Cuba. But Anne wanted to keep being a pirate, so she left it there with a nanny. And then this new pirate joined them, and it turned out *he* was a woman, too—Mary Read."

"No way," Dan said in disbelief. "You're telling me that a whole bunch of those old-time pirates were really women?"

Amy shook her head. "No, hardly any. It was just like this big coincidence that they both ended up on the same ship. And supposedly they were just as good fighters as any of the men—sometimes better."

She paused. *They could have been pals with Nellie. . . .*

"Calico Jack's ship got caught by the British Navy," Amy went on, "and the whole crew was put on trial. They were all found guilty and sentenced to death by hanging. But at the last minute, Anne and Mary told the court that they were pregnant. It was against the law to execute a pregnant woman, so they got sent to prison instead. And—"

"Let me guess," Dan said. "The prison is in Kingston?"

"No," Amy said, "it doesn't exist anymore."

"Then what are we going to Kingston for? This is an awfully long drive!"

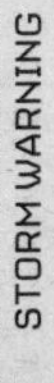

"The prison was in Spanish Town. That was the capital of Jamaica back then. But later they moved the capital and all the government records to Kingston. So that's why we're going there. To look up the records and see if there's anything that might help."

"Okay, I get it," Dan said. "But aren't you forgetting something?"

"What?"

"This." He tapped his chest.

Amy knew what "this" was. The bear claw. Dan was wearing the chain around his neck, and hopefully Nellie still didn't know about it.

"We don't have any idea how it fits in," Dan said. "It would make sense that some pirates were Tomas, all that adventuring and sword-fighting and stuff. And we found this in a Tomas cave. But it's like a dead end, it doesn't lead to anything else."

Amy sighed. "I've been worrying about that," she said. "We might end up having to go back to the Bahamas to hunt around some more. But the portrait with Anne Bonny's name on the back—that's a lead, too, and we know she was in Jamaica."

Amy took the little portrait out of her backpack. Together she and Dan leaned over it and studied the face with its wide green eyes and snub nose.

Hope.

Both marveled again that the woman in the picture looked just like their mother, Hope Cahill.

CHAPTER 8

They were in the wrong place. Again.

Nellie had parked at the Government Records Centre in Kingston. Within a few minutes, Dan and Amy learned from a clerk that they would have to backtrack to Spanish Town and go to the Jamaica Archives there. Fortunately, Spanish Town wasn't too far from Kingston.

The main square in Spanish Town was very impressive—beautiful old colonial buildings and lots of tall palm trees. The Jamaica Archives was a more modern two-story, tan-brick building just behind the square.

In the research room, Amy filled out the request form for the file she wanted to look at: the transcript for the trials of Jack Rackham, Anne Bonny, and Mary Read.

She gave the form to the man at the request desk. He was a tall, well-built young man with a name tag that read LESTER.

Lester stared at Nellie for a few moments; he seemed fascinated by her nose ring. She was busy untangling the cord to her earbuds and didn't seem to notice.

Then he glanced down at the form. "Oh, that file again," he said. "You Americans, you have a thing about pirates."

Amy caught her breath. "Has someone else been in here asking for this file lately?"

"Maybe not lately," he said. "Let's see—the record says it was last year sometime."

Amy frowned. That would have been before Grace's death—before this frenzied hunt for Clues started. Still, it could have been a Cahill. . . .

"Oh, and you know those *Pirates of the Caribbean* films?" Lester said. "They sent a researcher here and he looked up all our pirate stuff."

"Did they use anything they found?" Dan asked eagerly.

"Yah, they did, young man," he said with a smile. Amy thought it was a very nice smile, one that filled his whole face. Not just his mouth, but his cheeks and eyes, too. "Calico Jack Rackham was hanged, and then his body was squeezed into a little iron cage. They hung the cage at the entrance to Kingston Harbour with his rotting corpse as a warning to other pirates."

"Ewwww," Amy said.

"Cool!" Dan said.

Lester laughed. "In the movie, they changed it a little—they had pirates' corpses hanging from gallows instead of in a cage. But that's where they got the idea."

He got up and went into the stacks. A few minutes later, he returned with a file folder. Meanwhile, Nellie had wandered off toward an easy chair by the window. Lester stared at her again.

"I'll need a driver's license or passport to hold until you return the file," he said.

Dan went to Nellie and got her driver's license. Lester glanced at Nellie, then at the photo on the license, then back at Nellie again. Apparently satisfied, he put the license into a little numbered cubbyhole behind him and handed Amy the file.

In the chair by the window, Nellie was already dozing off. Amy and Dan sat down at a table nearby, split up the papers in the file, and began skimming through them. Or rather, Amy began skimming. Dan was still stuck on the rotten corpse.

"Do you think there were maggots?" he asked. "Probably. I mean, it's tropical here. He was probably *crawling* with them."

Amy hardly heard him. "Dan, listen to this," she said. "There's this witness testifying against Anne Bonny and Mary Read, who said that they wore 'Men's Jackets and long Trouzers, and Handkerchiefs tied about their heads.' And that 'the Reason of knowing and believing them to be Women then was, by the largeness of their Breasts.'"

"Um, that would do it," Dan said with a snicker. "But what happened to them? Were they in jail for the rest of their lives?"

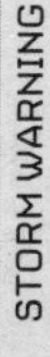

"Mary Read died in prison," Amy said, "only a few months later. But nobody knows for sure what happened to Anne. Some people think that her father—he was a big shot in South Carolina—managed to spirit her out of prison, and she lived under another name for the rest of her life."

Dan gave a little snort. "That sounds very Cahill-esque," he said.

"It's all pretty interesting," Amy said slowly, "but there's really nothing here that points to a clue." She nodded toward the papers she had given him. "What have you got there?"

"I don't know," he said. "It's a really long list. I started trying to read it, but it's just all this *stuff*."

Amy took the pages from him. Her heart skipped a beat. "Dan, do you realize what this is? It's the manifest of Rackham's ship!"

"Cool!" Dan said. Then, "What's a manifest?"

Amy was too excited even to roll her eyes at him. "It's like an inventory list of everything on board the ship when it was taken. Every ship had to have one by law."

"Even pirate ships? You'd think they'd be a little looser about rules like that."

"Actually, pirates were even stricter about it than some legitimate ships. The loot got divided up at the end of a trip, and of course every pirate wanted his fair share. So they kept really close track. When the quartermaster was making out the manifest, there had to be witnesses and everything. It was part of the pirates' code, and they were really proud of it."

The number and variety of things listed on the *William*'s manifest were astounding. The ship had been carrying all the equipment needed to make a life at sea. There was food: dried fish and salted meat; ship's biscuits, dried beans, salt, rum, and wine, as well as live chickens and turtles for slaughtering along the way. There were wooden trenchers for plates and leather pouches for cups. There were tools and weapons: axes, chisels, mallets, shovels; nets and fishing tackle; knives, cutlasses, pistols and muskets; powder, shot, cannons and cannonballs; leather vests for protection and metal cuirasses for even more protection. There were hammocks, ropes, canvas, chains; navigating instruments, maps, parchment paper, lanterns, needles, buckets, rags, jugs, surgical supplies and medicines. There were musical instruments—fiddle, flute, a concertina; checkers and chess sets and boards, playing cards and dice.

There was the ship's flag: Calico Jack's famous skull-and-crossbones. There was a cat, to keep the rats and mice at bay—and a parrot!

"What about doubloons?" Dan asked. "I thought pirate ships were always full of gold doubloons."

Amy flipped through the pages and found what she was looking for: the list of the booty taken from other ships.

"There's some gold here," she said, running her

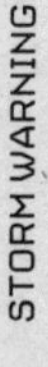

finger down the page. "Not a whole lot. They were sailing in a sloop, which was fast and easy to maneuver but couldn't carry as much cargo as a bigger, heavier ship."

Even so, the list was impressive.

24 Bolts Silk
15 Bolts Cotton, Madras & Calico
6 Silver Chargers
6 Silver Goblets
2 Doz. Silver Spoons
4 Pewter Flasks
8 Silver Bowls
1 Silver Tea Service
1 Pewter Coffee Service
4 Bags Silver Coins
2 Bags Gold Coins
1 Leather Pouch Containing 98 Pearls
2 Gold Bands, plain
1 Gold Band, carved
7 Gold Chains
1 Pendant, Lion Head, ruby eyes
1 Silver Moon pendant
1 Cameo Brooch, Carved, Onyx Stone
1 Gold Cross, carved
2 Silver Crosses, plain
1 Serpent Medallion, Carved, Green Stone
1 Floral Medallion, Gold, Sapphires
3 Brooches, Gold

2 Brooches, Gold & Gems
3 Brooches, Silver, Carved
3 Snuffboxes, Silver
2 Snuffboxes, Silver Inlaid
2 Silver-handled Mirrors
2 Ivory Combs
4 Tortoise-Shell Combs
1 Ivory-handled Mirror
2 Silver Hair-Pins with Pearls
1 Gold Hair-Pin, Plain
10 Crates Tobacco
10 Barrels Sugar
3 Sacks Pepper Corns
2 Sacks Nutmegs
1 Sack Mace
14 Deer Hides
6 Buffalo Hides
1 Crate Beaver Furs
3 Gilded Talons, Panther, Bear, Eagle
1 Ivory Whale-Tusk, Carved
Antlers of Large Deer
Animal Jawbones With Teeth, Buffalo, Bearcat, Wolf
2 Doz. Pea-Cock Feathers
8 Ostrich Plumes
26 Turkey Quills
6 Large Conch Shells
1 Silver Chest, Small, Carved
3 Wooden Chests, Large, Brass-Trimmed
4 Doz. Tobacco Pipes, Clay

Almost without her realizing it, Amy's finger went back up the list and stopped; it was as if she were developing invisible antennae for anything connected to the hunt for Clues. "Dan, listen," she said. "'Three Gilded Talons, Panther, Bear, Eagle.'"

Dan grinned and patted his chest, where the bear claw hung safely beneath his shirt. "Yup," he said. "Proves that Calico Jack and Anne whatshername really knew about this."

But Amy was already focused on the manifest again. Another listing had caught her eye.

"'Animal Jawbones With Teeth, Buffalo, Bearcat, Wolf,'" she read aloud. She looked up in excitement. "Wolf, Dan! The Janus symbol!"

Dan looked dubious. "Uh, don't you think that might be stretching it a little? I mean, 'bearcat' would maybe make sense, too. Bear for Tomas, and maybe Hamilton *was* saying 'cat' after all. Is there such a thing as a calico bearcat?"

Amy snorted. "If there is, I've never heard of it."

A wolf jawbone as a Janus hint? Dan was probably right—maybe that was stretching it; it was enough to have found proof that the bear claw really was something associated with Anne Bonny.

"Wait," Dan said, staring at the page. "I think I just changed my mind."

He pointed to a line on the manifest:

1 Serpent Medallion, Carved, Green Stone

"Serpent?" Amy said. "As in, snakes, for Lucian?

"Nope," he said.

"How can you be so sure?"

"Because"—he cocked his head smugly—"we've already got this one."

Amy looked at him, completely at a loss. He tortured her with silence for a few moments longer, then said, "In fact, I believe you're *wearing* it as we speak."

Her mouth fell open as her hand flew to her neck.

Grace's necklace!

She took it off so they could examine it. The medallion was shaped like a rectangle with rounded corners. The dragon was carved in full relief on one side of the jade; the reverse side was plain except for its smooth beveled edges.

Dan was grinning. "Serpent—dragon. Green stone—green jade. Carved medallion—carved medallion. Am I right or am I right?" he said.

Amy closed her eyes to focus on the thought that was forming in her mind.

"Okay," she said slowly. "Suppose Anne Bonny was a Cahill. That's not so far-fetched. To start with, she was born in Ireland, where the original Cahills lived. And then there's the portrait." She didn't need to elaborate further; Dan would know she was thinking about Anne's uncanny resemblance to their mother.

"She lived during a time when women were really restricted. Most of them weren't allowed to do a lot of the things that men could. Like travel. So she finds out about the clues, and she disguises herself as a man and becomes a pirate because she figures it'll be the best way to hunt for clues."

She opened her eyes to see Dan listening intently.

"Or hide them," he said. "Dragon medallion, bear claw—that's why I think you might be right after all, about the wolf."

Amy began scanning the manifest again. "But there's nothing here about snakes," she said, disappointed.

Dan seemed unfazed. "That doesn't matter. She might not have found a snake thing yet. Or she found it already and hid it somewhere." Then he frowned. "But we still have the same problem. We've got an Ekat symbol and a Tomas symbol. What are they for? And what do we do now?"

"That's easy. We keep following Anne Bonny's trail," Amy said. She wished she felt as confident as she sounded; in truth, it was the only thing she could think of. "The prison is gone now, but I thought we'd look around anyway. It was right here in Spanish Town. Maybe there's a memorial or something there."

They copied down the entire manifest. Then they gave the file back to Lester, who returned Nellie's license to them.

As they went to wake Nellie, both of them fingered their neckpieces.

Amy, the jade dragon. Dan, the gilded bear claw.

CHAPTER 9

Nellie had the feeling that someone was following her.

They were walking through the parking lot of the Archives building. She glanced over her shoulder.

She was right but relaxed immediately. It was only that guy Lester.

"Please, young lady," he said to Nellie, "will you come with me?"

Nellie stopped, turned, looked him over. She'd been so tired from all the driving that she hadn't taken much notice of him earlier.

Tall, muscular, in a short-sleeved shirt that fit him very nicely. And that Jamaican accent, so cool. *Pretty fine*, Nellie thought.

"I'm busy at the moment," she said, and nodded toward Dan and Amy. "But"—she smiled, tilted her head, and blinked slowly—"maybe later?"

Standing off to the side with Amy, Dan mimed putting a finger down his throat.

"I'm afraid it has to be now," he said firmly.

Nellie frowned. “I said *later,* but I think I’m changing my mind.”

He held up his hands and took a step back. “Hey, ease up, sister. You just need to come with me because somebody wants to talk to you.”

Nellie frowned. *Who could that possibly be? If it were McIntyre or—or the other guy, they would just call or e-mail, they wouldn’t send a message through someone else. . . .*

She tried to disguise her puzzlement by talking tough. “If they want to talk to me, they can talk to me right here, like you are,” she said. “I’m not going with someone I don’t know to talk to someone else I don’t know when I don’t know where I’m going or—most important—*why.*”

Lester was silent for a moment. Then he said, “Yah, I get that you’re nervous. How about this. I’ll take you to the street. You can check it out. There are people all around, you can see that it’s safe. You stand outside the house and she’ll come out to talk to you. She’s old, but that much she can do. Okay?”

Nellie pointed her chin at Dan and Amy. “I don’t go anywhere without them.”

Lester shrugged. “She didn’t say anything about other people. It’s fine with me.”

They set out with Lester leading the way. He turned off the big avenue onto a smaller street. As he had promised, there were still plenty of people around. After a couple of blocks, he stopped in front of a small bungalow that had once been painted pink but was now faded to a weak shade of tan. He led them up the shallow concrete steps to the front porch.

"You wait here," he said. He opened the screen door and went inside. They heard him call out, "Granma? A dawta here to you."

Dan and Amy looked startled. "Daughter—?" Dan said.

"Patois," Nellie said. "Jamaicans speak standard English to tourists but patois to each other. 'Dawta' means 'daughter,' but it can also mean 'woman,' especially a younger woman. So he said something like, 'a young woman here to see you.'"

"How do you know all that?" Amy demanded.

"I have Jamaican friends in Boston," Nellie said. "I used to go to reggae clubs with them." It was the truth, but Amy didn't look entirely convinced.

"What is your problem?" Nellie said with an impatient flap of her hand. "It's not like I could learn every language in the world just to spy on you guys! And even if I was going to try, do you think Jamaican patois would be high on the list?"

No reply, of course. *Amy, always scared of her own shadow . . . who'd have thought she could be so stubborn?*

The door opened. Standing there was a very old woman, bony, dark-skinned and gray-haired, wearing glasses. She looked at Nellie, expressionless, and nodded.

Then she flicked a glance at Dan and finally at Amy. Her eyes lit up.

"Ha!" she said.

All three of them jumped.

"Look pon Grace!" the old woman said to Amy, and laughed heartily.

Nellie was now thoroughly confused. Lester had wanted *her* to come with him, but now the old woman seemed to recognize Amy. What was going on?

"Me shoulda know." The woman shook her head, still smiling. "You fayva Grace a whole heap. Dem eyes, uh-huh, yes."

Amy cleared her throat. "You—you knew my grandmother?"

"Jah know, dat is one fine lady. How she do now?"

It was Dan who answered. "Our grandmother died," he said. "In August."

The light faded from the woman's eyes. "Hush, bwoy. I so sorry. Sorry, sorry, sorry. I nebah know."

Awkward silence.

"It's okay," Nellie said at last. It wasn't, but what were you supposed to say at a time like this?

"Yes," the woman said. "Is her time. Nobody cyant do nothin' when is their time." A pause. "My name Alice—you to call me Miss Alice."

"I'm Nellie, and this is Dan and Amy."

"I am surprise, seein' Grace's girl there," Miss Alice said. "But *you* is de one I waitin' on." She jerked her chin at Nellie.

"Me? But how—I didn't—you couldn't—"

"Grace. She say you gwine come one day, tell me to look out for you."

"She told you that? When?"

Miss Alice wrinkled her forehead. "She here when . . . twenty year ago? Maybe goin' on for twenty-five now."

Nellie turned toward the porch steps. "Okay, we're out of here," she said. "I don't know what your game is, Miss Alice, but I know for sure that the truth isn't part of it. I wasn't even *born* then, and I didn't meet Grace until this year."

Miss Alice scowled. "Ease up, dawta. You always so rude to them who is older than you?"

Nellie felt like a little kid, getting scolded like that. She hesitated, trying to decide on a response.

"Siddung, lemme finish." Miss Alice glared at her, then limped to a battered lawn chair and sat down. Dan and Amy sat on the porch steps. Nellie took the other chair but didn't plan on getting too comfortable. Miss Alice waited a moment, then went on.

"Grace come lookin' for me. Not me, 'zactly, but she lookin' for sint'in' I got. Sint'in' been in de fambly long time. She find it, meaning to say she find *me,* an' she aks a favor. She say, when someone come with de matchin' piece, I am to give mine to them."

Miss Alice made that sharp short laugh again. "Ha! I say, why I should do like she say? She a stranger, and this in my fambly for how long I don' know. But you know Grace, she don' give up."

Amy and Dan nodded at her and at each other.

"She tell me it important to her and *her* fambly, den aks me what do I want, what she to give me, 'f I do dat for her. An' I think on it a long time, long time. Two, three months. She stay right yah-so, visit me every day. We talk about Jamaica, she want to know all de old stories. She a give me time to think on it. And 'tween times we get to be frens.

"So I finally mek up my mind and I tell her, what I want is, Lester to get educated. College. He jus' a pickney then, no bigger dan dis"—she held her hand up at knee height—"but we not stoosh, get by all right, but college cost too dear.

"An' Grace say fine and lef, back to the States. But she call from time to time, memba me, memba Lester. Time come, Lester go a college in Atlanta, get hisself a fancy degree, an' now a good job. He study history and liberryin'."

Miss Alice nodded. "Yes. So den I must keep dat promise I mek. Grace dint say no rude American girl a come," she said with a sniff. "Jus' whoever come with de match."

"What match?" Nellie asked, mystified.

Miss Alice turned her head. "Lester!" she shouted. "Bring me dat box in de drawer 'side my bed."

Lester came out to the porch with a sandwich in one hand and a small box in the other.

"Lester, meet dem folks," Miss Alice said. "Dey is Denny an' Ellie an' Jamie."

"Close enough," Nellie said under her breath.

"Lester sight you," Miss Alice said. "I don't get round much no more, so long time ago I told him what to look for. He see you at de archives, den call me." She beamed at him proudly.

Lester gave them that nice smile and handed Miss Alice the box. "Me going now, Granma," he said. They made their good-byes, and Lester left, still munching on his sandwich.

Miss Alice gave the box a little shake. "All dem years," she said. Then she peered closely at Nellie through her glasses. "Yah, is a match, alright."

Nellie was beside herself with curiosity. *The match to what—my face?* she wondered. It was all she could do to keep herself from snatching the box out of the old woman's hands.

Dan stood up from the step. Amy edged forward.

Miss Alice lifted the lid of the box and removed a protective layer of cotton fluff. She stretched out her hand.

They all leaned forward to see what rested inside.

A small silver snake.

The identical twin to the one Nellie wore in her nose.

CHAPTER 10

"You order for me," Nellie said to Amy.

For the first time on the entire trip, Nellie didn't look at the menu. Her mind was too preoccupied to think about food.

They had stayed at Miss Alice's house for a couple of hours; it had taken that long to hear the whole story.

Hundreds of years earlier, an ancestor of Miss Alice's had worked as a nanny for a woman in Cuba. The woman put her baby in the nanny's care and also gave the nanny a pair of silver snake earrings. She told her to keep both the baby and the earrings safe.

The woman then left Cuba to join her husband. At sea.

They were pirates.

The baby died in infancy. The nanny was so distraught that she made a vow to take care of those earrings no matter what. Over the years, one of the earrings had gotten lost. But Miss Alice's family had faithfully guarded the remaining earring. Everywhere they went, they brought the little silver snake with them. It had been passed down, mother to daughter, for nearly three hundred years.

In some impossible way, Grace had discovered that the second earring had ended up in Mexico, with another branch of the family. It, too, had been faithfully passed down. A generation ago, there had been no daughters born to that family, so the earring was passed to a son. When he grew up and had children of his own, he gave the earring to his oldest daughter.

Nellie.

Now Nellie rubbed the back of her neck with one hand. She could feel knots of tension in her muscles.

"If Grace traced the earring to my family, she must have had her eye on me for *years,*" she said. "But she never said a word about it. Why didn't she tell me?"

"Well," Amy said, "now you know how it feels."

Nellie stared. "What are you talking about?"

"You didn't tell us the whole truth, just like what Grace did to you."

Nellie felt the blood rush to her face. "It's not the same thing at all!"

Amy raised an eyebrow. "You don't think?"

Her calmness made Nellie even madder. "I'm talking about my whole life here!" she said, pounding the table with her fist. "Everything! Like—like—what about the flying lessons?"

"Flying lessons?" Dan said, clearly mystified by the change in subject.

"They're expensive, right? But my dad said no problem. Did Grace pay for them? Come to think of it, it wasn't even my idea—it was *his*! Or maybe it was Grace's, and does that mean my parents were in on the whole thing all along?" Nellie caught her breath in what was almost a sob. "This isn't just about the stupid clues thing. This is *my family*!"

Amy looked at her for a long moment. "For the last few months," she said slowly, "*our* family has been the three of us."

Her sentence hung in the air almost as if it were written there.

Nellie looked at their faces, both as solemn as she'd ever seen them.

It's true, Nellie thought. *Parents gone, grandmother gone, an aunt who doesn't want them.* Guilt washed over her yet again—for lying to them and even more, over her part in what was soon to happen. . . .

She slumped forward, her head in her hands. "Okay, I get it," she said quietly. "I thought I did before, but now I *really* get it. How you felt—still feel, I guess—about me working for Grace and McIntyre. You feel like you've been played, and that's what I feel like now, too."

The silence among them grew to awkward proportions. They were rescued by the waiter, who arrived with the three plates of jerk chicken Amy had ordered.

Nellie was suddenly ravenous. She began attacking her chicken. It was delicious.

"Dude," she said. "This is *good.*"

Spicy, but not just pepper-hot. Thyme, for sure . . . maybe nutmeg, too? And mace? She'd have to look up a recipe and make it herself sometime.

Dan's mouth wasn't quite full as he spoke. "C'we talk 'bout shomething elsh now?" he said.

"Swallow," Amy commanded.

Nellie's phone rang. She took it out of her pack and looked at it.

"It's my dad," she said. She had left a message for him when they were at Miss Alice's house; she wanted to tell him about their newfound relative.

And now she had other things to talk about. She stood up from the table and walked outside to take the call.

A few minutes later, she came back to the table, shaking her head. "That Grace. She never quits."

"What? What is it?" Amy and Dan said at the same time.

"My dad got a letter from Grace. A few weeks before she passed away. He thought the letter was kinda strange because it was so short. It just said that if I ever found the mate to my snake, he should give me a message."

"What message? What was the message?" The sibling chorus again.

Nellie frowned a little. "The message is even shorter. 'C/o The Right Excellent Nanny,'" she said. "The c/o, that means 'care of,' which is weird—you only ever see it as part of a mailing address."

"'The Right Excellent Nanny,'" Amy echoed. "Wow. Grace planned for you to be the one to find the missing earring all along."

The waiter came by to give them the check. He poured more water for them.

"Yeah, but it doesn't really sound like Grace, does it?" Dan said. "Too—too awkward, or something. 'The Right Excellent Nanny,' hmmm . . . "

The waiter paused in his water pouring. "Oh, yah," he said. "You already been to the park?"

All three of them looked at him blankly.

"Heroes Park," he said. "Her statue there."

Then they looked at each other blankly. Nellie recovered first. "Whose statue where?"

Now he looked at *them* blankly. "Nanny," he said. "You talkin' about Nanny of the Maroons, yah? The Right Excellent Nanny?"

"That's somebody's *name*?" Nellie said, incredulous.

"One of our Jamaican heroes," he said. "Go see the National Heroes Park. In Kingston."

All three of them jumped up from their chairs.

Back to Kingston again. In the car, Amy and Dan had a quick whispered powwow. Then Amy climbed into the front seat.

"No earbuds required," she announced. "We've decided that since Grace intended this hint for you, we might need you to be in on it."

Nellie nodded.

"We don't know exactly what we're looking for," Amy said carefully. Even though they had decided to include Nellie in this stage of the hunt, Amy still didn't want to give away too much. "But it might be something Janus. We think maybe Nanny was a Janus."

"So it could be something to do with a wolf," Dan added. "Maybe, like, a fang. That would be awesome—a big ol' wolf fang!"

Honestly, the things boys think are awesome . . . "You'd probably love it if it had drool all over it," Amy said. Then she changed the subject before it could get any grosser. "Laptop, please?"

For the rest of the drive she researched The Right Excellent Nanny. Nanny Sharpe, known as Queen Nanny or Granny Nanny, had been captured in West Africa and brought to Jamaica as a slave. But she and her brothers escaped. High in the mountains of Jamaica, they established communities for runaway slaves, called Maroons. When the British finally found them, Nanny led the fight to keep from being enslaved again.

"She had all kinds of warfare strategies," Amy said. "She made sure the towns only had one point of entry, like up high on a cliff, so they could control who came in and out. And—oh, you'll like this—she had her

Maroons put leaves and branches on their clothes. Then they'd hide until the Brits were practically on top of them and spring a surprise attack. It says here in one battle, the Maroons were seriously outnumbered but still managed to kill all but one British soldier."

Nellie grinned. "Dude, I am lovin' this. First a girl pirate, and now this Nanny. It's great, isn't it?" she said as she glanced at Amy.

"What's so great about it?" Dan asked.

"Women," Nellie answered. "Women kicking butt all over the place."

The entrance to the National Heroes Park was pretty grand for a laid-back island like Jamaica, with a big war memorial statue guarded by soldiers in fancy uniforms. A few minutes' walk to the eastern side of the park brought them to a triad of tall metal sculptures, each as high as a flagpole. Dan ran ahead to read the plaque in front of the sculptures.

"This is it!" he yelled.

The girls hurried to join him.

MONUMENT TO
THE RIGHT EXCELLENT NANNY OF THE MAROONS

"Maybe it's some kind of code," Dan said doubtfully.

Amy pointed to the nearest sculpture. It was topped by a large metal horn that looked like an empty Thanksgiving cornucopia.

"That horn," she said. "I read about it on one of the websites. It's called an *abeng*. It's from the Ashanti tribe in Ghana. In Africa. That's where Nanny was from. She used it to warn her warriors during battle."

The sculpture was constructed to be heard as well as seen. When the wind blew, the horn made a faint but eerie sound, almost like a wail.

Dan cocked his head, listening for a moment. Then he grinned. "That sound means it's *hollow.*"

Amy gasped. "Something could be inside!"

All three of them ran to the base of the sculpture. The pole itself was made of metal, twisted evenly so it looked sort of like a rope. "I always wanted to climb a flagpole," Dan said eagerly.

Amy glanced around. There were a few people walking nearby, but nobody official looking.

"How do you think I should do this?" Dan asked.

"I saw these guys on TV, in the tropics somewhere, who gather coconuts," Nellie said. "They looped a rope around the trunk and used it to climb up."

"Fine," Dan said. "Rope, please."

None of them had a rope, of course.

Dan snapped his fingers. He took out his phone, dialed a number, and waited.

"Who are you calling?" Amy asked.

He held up one finger.

"Hey, Hamilton, it's me," Dan said. "Got a question for you. Ever climbed a flagpole?"

CHAPTER 11

Hamilton Holt, it turned out, was a flagpole-climbing champ. Part of his dad's training regimen for the family, he explained to Dan, was climbing all manner of obstacles. Dan received detailed instructions in exchange for a promise to tell Hamilton what, if anything, was inside the horn.

"I don't know—" Amy said doubtfully.

"It's worth the risk," Dan argued. "There might be nothing inside. And even if there *is* something, I didn't promise to give it to him, only to tell him what it is."

He reviewed Hamilton's instructions. "Ham said that if the pole's metal, clothes make you slip." He pulled off his T-shirt.

Nellie's eyes widened. "So you're supposed to take off all your clothes?"

"Are you out of your mind?" Dan said. "I'm not climbing this thing naked!"

"I didn't say that—*you* said—"

"He said to wear sneakers and strip down as much

as possible," Dan said. "I don't think I have to be *completely* naked."

Nellie covered her mouth with her hand and turned away; Amy cleared her throat several times. Both of them were clearly hiding giggles. *So* immature. He decided to ignore them for the moment.

"I'm supposed to keep my body as close to the pole as I can by wrapping my legs around it." Dan said. "Then I reach up with my hands, reposition my feet, and hike myself higher."

"Be careful," Amy said. She and Nellie stood on opposite sides of the base of the sculpture.

Dan took one last look at the horn. Then he grabbed the pole, wrapped his legs around it, and began pulling himself up a little at a time.

The ridges of the twisted pole dug into his sunburned legs, making him wince.

After about six inches of progress, he let go and dropped back down to the ground.

"Okay," he said, flexing his fingers and hands. It hurt to grip so hard. "I've got the feel of it." He gazed again at the top of the pole; the horn suddenly looked much farther away. "It's harder than I thought."

"Want me to try?" Nellie asked.

"No, thanks, I'll give it another shot." He felt almost insulted by the offer.

"If we gave you a boost, you could start up higher," Amy suggested.

With some maneuvering, several grunts, and more

than one "ouch," they managed to get Dan standing with one foot on Nellie's shoulder and the other on Amy's, holding on to the pole.

"Way better," he said. He was now already almost halfway to the top. Cautiously, he took his right foot off Amy's shoulder and wrapped his leg around the pole.

"Here I go," he said, and took his left foot off Nellie.

Hands—feet—hands—feet . . . Hamilton had said to keep an even rhythm. It was almost like Dan's hands started looking forward to the tiny rest they got when he let go to move them up farther. In what seemed like almost no time, he reached the top.

"I did it!" he called down to the girls.

First mistake. He was much higher than he'd expected! It wasn't like being in a plane or on top of a building—there was nothing keeping him in the air but his own muscle power.

Dan gulped. *Okay, so don't look down again,* he told himself firmly.

"Look in the horn!" Amy was calling back. "Do you see anything?"

Now things got tricky. He was right up against the *side* of the horn. The flared opening jutted out from the pole almost an arm's length. There was no way he could look into the opening.

"I can't look into it," he said. "I'm just going to have to try to reach in."

He held on with his left hand and stretched out his right. Gingerly, he put his hand inside.

Nothing but the horn's metal interior.

He adjusted his grip on the pole and reached in a little farther. Then he felt something else—prickly? No, *crawly* . . .

"YIKES!" he shouted.

With a panicked motion of his hand, he swept out whatever it was he had just touched and flung it toward the ground.

Amy knew what it was as soon as she saw it falling. She knew because it was her secret nightmare: She would recognize it instantly, anywhere.

Sharks, scary. Venomous snakes, scary. Huge spiders, scary. But for Amy, this particular creature was beyond scary. It wasn't just frightening. It was almost . . . evil.

Amy knew this was irrational. Animals weren't evil. They were what they were, and maybe she should even admire this one. It had been in existence for millions of years, surviving when other species had been unable to adapt. But she couldn't help it. Her fear seemed to come from so deep inside it was part of her DNA—a complete and instinctive kind of fear.

She could hardly have seen more than its color and size—dark and small—as it fell through the air when the word exploded in her mind.

Scorpion!

As Amy watched in utter horror, the scorpion fell onto Nellie's head, bounced once, and landed on her back, just below her shoulder.

"Nellie," she whispered.

It wasn't even really a whisper; she had barely moved her lips.

Amy felt a familiar panic. The kind where she would end up frozen, unable to move or speak.

NO! she yelled at herself. *DON'T FREEZE—move something, anything!*

She clenched and unclenched her fists. Just once, but somehow it seemed to help. She could almost feel the blood moving through her hands and arms and up into her body.

Now she forced her voice out of hiding. "Nellie," she said. "Do. Not. Move."

Amy crouched down and picked up the T-shirt Dan had thrown on the ground. Then she tiptoed toward Nellie.

She could see the scorpion clearly now. It was only a few inches long but still positively evil looking, tail curved over its back, pincers raised.

Amy grasped the shirt with both hands. *Deep breath . . .*

She slammed her hands together so the fabric closed around the scorpion. She squeezed hard and felt something crunch and squish. Then she flung the shirt away as far as she could and collapsed onto the ground.

Nellie broke out of statue mode immediately. "Dude," she said, "what was *that*?"

Amy could hardly breathe. "S-scorpion," she gasped. "I don't know if—if I killed it—"

Nellie walked over to the shirt and peered at it cautiously from a safe distance.

"Ew," she said. Then she grinned at Amy. "He's a goner." She picked up the shirt and shook out the bits of dead scorpion. "Thanks, kiddo."

Amy swallowed.

"Anytime," she said shakily.

"Hey," Dan hollered from the top of the pole. "It's just me up here, all alone. Everybody okay down there?"

"Yeah," Nellie said. "Your sister just killed a scorpion."

"No way," Dan said.

"Way," Nellie replied. "What's going on up there?"

"One more try," Dan said. "I sure hope that scorpion didn't live with a whole bunch of relatives."

He held on to the pole with his right hand and freed his left, wiggling his fingers to keep them from cramping. Then he grabbed on again.

"There better be—I don't know, *rubies* or something in there," he said.

Grimly, he plunged his hand into the horn one more time.

Nothing crawly. Good.

Nothing at all. Bad.

"If there's anything in here, I can't reach it," he called without looking down. "It's sort of like, dusty. I can feel a little grit. But that's all."

He pulled his hand out. It was very dirty. And his other arm was killing him.

Dan closed his eyes for a moment and tried to concentrate. The horn was hollow. . . . How could you hide something inside a plain empty space like that? It wasn't like the cave, there weren't any rocks to put something under—

Wait. It *was* like the cave in a way. The mouth of the horn was like the opening of the cave . . . and Amy had found the Tomas sign inside above the opening. . . .

Dan hiked himself up the pole a few more inches. Then he groped around just inside the horn's mouth. At the top, he felt some kind of ridge in the metal—maybe a seam where it had been welded together? With his fingertips he traced the ridge.

It was a skinny strip of metal nearly half the circumference of the horn, eight or nine inches long, maybe a little longer.

He picked at one corner with his fingernail. The strip was *not* welded to the horn—the corner came free as he picked at it. It was stuck to the horn with some kind of adhesive.

"Please please please," Dan whispered fiercely.

Bit by bit, he pried off the strip. It was not until the

whole strip was free that he realized how numb his other arm was.

"I'm coming down now," he called. Then he grinned. "And I'm not alone."

"YES!" Amy raised her arms in triumph.

It was a strip of gold, soft enough to have taken on the curve of the horn and bent at one corner where Dan had pried it up. Close up, they could see that it was actually two strips of metal welded into one.

"But it isn't anything to do with a wolf," Dan said, disappointed.

"That's okay," Amy said doggedly. "It's still obviously something to do with the clue hunt."

There were raised letters embossed on the whole length of the strip on both sides—letters so tiny that they were impossible to read. All three of them tried; Dan was the only one who thought he could make out a few letters.

"I see some Os, they're easy," he said. "And maybe some Ms? Or they could be Ws."

"I have a little magnifying mirror in the car," Nellie said.

As they walked to the parking lot, Dan put his T-shirt back on.

"Yuck," Nellie said, pointing at the front of it.

Dan looked down at the smears and stains. "Cool," he said. "Scorpion guts!"

CHAPTER 12

True to his word, Dan phoned Hamilton to tell him what they had found. This time, the connection was terrible, which turned out to work in their favor; it was clear that Hamilton couldn't make heads or tails of the conversation. But Amy agreed with Dan that they had held up their side of the deal.

Now they were in the car, examining the gold strip with a magnifying mirror that Nellie produced from her luggage.

"First four letters e-k-t-o," Dan said.

"Ekto," Nellie said. "That's from Greek. It means 'outer,' or 'outside.' Then m-a-l, right? 'Mal,' French, with Latin roots, meaning 'bad.'" She frowned. "After that, 'u-j-a,' and the whole thing starts over again. But I don't know what 'uja' means."

"J-A for Jamaica?" Dan proposed. "And U, short for Y-O-U. Outside, bad, you, Jamaica?"

"Too late," Amy said. "We've already been outside a lot here."

Something about the letters seemed vaguely familiar to her. . . . What was it?

"'Ekto' and 'mal' do sound like some kind of warning," Nellie said. "It would probably make sense if we knew what 'uja' meant."

Amy felt a sharp pang. *The three of us working together—that's what it was like before. And now it's all different, and we'll never be able to trust her again, not like before. . . .*

SCRRREEEEEECH!

Amy jerked her head up. A big SUV was pulling into the parking lot much too fast.

Dan started yelling. "GO, NELLIE! DRIVE—GET OUT OF HERE NOW!"

Nellie obeyed instantly, jerking the car into gear and heading for the lot's exit. She peeled out into traffic, causing cars going both ways to slam on their brakes. The driver of the SUV had to wait for the traffic to untangle before making the turn behind them.

"What—?" Amy said.

"Cobras," Dan said grimly.

The Kabras had followed them to Jamaica.

By dint of very creative driving, some of which may not have been entirely legal, Nellie managed to lose the SUV in downtown Kingston. Now they were in an alley behind a sporting goods store, hiding out.

"I've had it up to *here* with them!" Dan said angrily. "It's always them chasing us. Why can't it be *us* chasing *them,* just for once?"

Amy's lips were pale. "We—we have to stay away from them," she whispered. "Especially Isabel."

"I'm with you there," Nellie said. "Let's see"—she started ticking off on her fingers—"Amy and the sharks, snakes in the mine, the fire in Indonesia, all three of us in the airplane hangar. What do you think she'll do for an encore?"

Amy hesitated. Then she said quietly, "You forgot one."

Nellie saw the expression on Dan's face change from anger to anguish. Amy closed her eyes.

Their parents, Nellie thought. Years ago, when Amy was seven and Dan only four, Isabel Kabra had deliberately, coldheartedly, started the fire in which Hope Cahill and Arthur Trent had died.

Of course, Nellie had known this for ages. But it was only at certain moments that it really hit her. She tried to imagine what it would be like to know that the person who murdered your parents was free in the world—and gunning for you as well.

"That *witch,*" she said bitterly. "I mean, anyone who would threaten to throw a kid into an ocean full of sharks—"

Suddenly, Amy opened her eyes, and Nellie could almost feel the electricity of excitement crackling from her.

"She has it," Amy announced. "The Janus icon."

When Amy had closed her eyes, she was doing her best to block out the image of her parents' death. Even the memory of being on that boat in Australia with Isabel was better than thinking about how Mom and Dad had died. . . .

It was a sound, not a picture, that came to her first. A small metallic sound, like something rattling, almost tinkling.

Isabel's bracelet. It was sliding around her wrist as she gestured at the water. A gold bracelet.

Amy hadn't thought anything of it at the time, of course; she'd been too busy being terrified. But now the image grew clearer.

The charms . . . Like a camera lens zooming in, Amy's memory homed in on one charm in particular. Triangular, with a sharp point . . . She could see it in her mind's eye with perfect clarity.

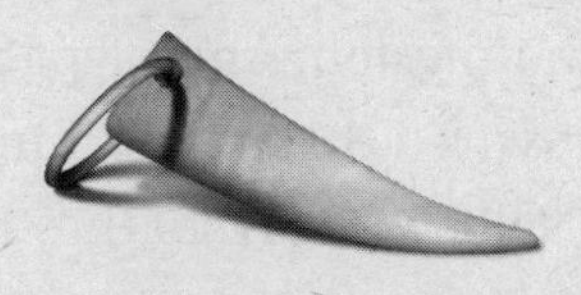

She blinked in sudden realization. "We were right," she said. "Remember the manifest? The animal bones?"

"It's a jawbone?" Dan said in amazement. "A wolf's jaw?"

Amy shook her head. "Not the whole jaw," she said. "One tooth—a fang, just like you wanted. And we're going to steal it from her."

Planning an ambush was hard work.

"Excellent Nanny probably had *weeks* to work out her ambushes," Dan complained. "We could definitely use her help."

The Cahills got busy. They chose the location after a quick stop at the tourist information office: a forested park outside Kingston, where a ropes course was being constructed near a waterfall. They spent the afternoon checking out the park and buying a little equipment.

Over her (very loud) protests, Nellie was made to stay in the car during the reconnaissance of the park. Amy had been firm about this.

"This has nothing to do with Grace's letter, so you're out of the loop again. We'll need you standing by with the car so we can get out of there at the end. That's it." Nothing Nellie said would change her mind.

At a hotel in Kingston, Amy slept badly that night, exhausted but wired. In the morning, she could see on Dan's and Nellie's faces that they hadn't slept well, either. But they couldn't wait any longer. They had to find the Kabras before the Kabras found them.

After breakfast, Amy nodded at Nellie. "Make the call," she said.

"Since when did you become CEO?" Nellie muttered. She punched in the number.

Irony. That was the right word. Amy knew that McIntyre had some kind of line to their rivals, and Nellie had a line to McIntyre. Nellie's betrayal had become a tool that the Cahills were now using to try to gain an advantage.

Nellie spoke briefly into the phone and told McIntyre to get a message to the Kabras.

Then they packed the car and drove to the park.

Nellie was in the car on the road beyond the park's entrance. Dan sat with Amy at a picnic table off the side of the path that led into the forest, screened by a stand of trees.

The Kabras were right on schedule. Their now-familiar SUV pulled into the dirt parking lot of the forest preserve. Isabel got out of the driver's seat and walked toward the path, followed by Ian and Natalie.

Dan's heart was in his throat. During all their other confrontations with Isabel, they'd been running away. This was different. This time, they wanted her here.

He licked his lips. Futilely, as it turned out—his mouth was all but spitless. "Ready?" he croaked.

Amy had that scared-rabbit look in her eyes, but she nodded. He saw her clench and unclench her fists.

Dan exhaled once, hard. Then, feigning surprise, he jumped to his feet.

"Amy! Kabras—RUN!" he yelled.

They ran up the path about a quarter mile until it forked into two smaller tracks. Dan veered to the left while Amy went right. As they split up, Dan risked a quick look over his shoulder.

All three Kabras were chasing them. Isabel Kabra was running flat out, her children barely keeping up.

"Ian! Go after the boy!" Isabel shouted.

Dan was panting up a steep slope now. Soon he reached a sign posted along the dirt track:

COMING SOON!
BLUE MOUNTAIN ROPES COURSE
FUN AND ADVENTURE FOR THE WHOLE FAMILY!

The ropes course had several stations spread out over a few acres. A couple of men were working on the last stations, but the beginning of the course was finished—and deserted.

Now Dan pounded down the path for several yards until it opened onto a little clearing. There was a rough, newly built hut on the left, and to the right, the first station of the ropes course: wooden slats nailed ladder fashion to the trunk of a big tree.

It was straight out of Nanny's book. The ladder was the only point of entry to the ropes course.

Halfway up the ladder, Dan checked to see that Ian was still following. For the plan to work, he had to make sure Ian didn't lose him. Dan heard footsteps and hard breathing; satisfied, he kept climbing.

About sixty feet above the ground was a small wooden platform. A heavy metal cable led to a second platform in another tree. Half a dozen pulleys were rigged to the cable. The pulleys had large metal clips on them, meant to be fastened to harnesses. With no harness, Dan grabbed the clip itself.

When Ian entered the clearing and spotted him, Dan launched himself into the air, hanging on to the clip for dear life. He'd done it earlier, when they checked out the place, so he already knew what it would feel like.

If Ian hadn't been chasing him, riding the zip line would have been one of the most fun things Dan had ever done. Actually, it was *still* pretty fun. For the few moments it took to zip down the line, he didn't think about Isabel or the Madrigals or the Clue hunt; he just held on tight as he sped through the air, the sky rushing by above him and the ground far below.

Dan landed on the second platform and looked back. Right on cue, Ian was following him up the ladder.

The next station was another zip line. Then Dan crossed the third obstacle, a rope bridge that stretched across a dry gully. Ahead he could see the landing platform and beyond it, a long expanse of cargo net.

As he began climbing the cargo net, Dan muttered a fervent plea. "Please please let this work. . . ."

The cargo net was in two sections that ascended at about a forty-five-degree angle. The first section ended at a horizontal bar set between two trees. Then a second stretch hung from several hooks underneath the next landing platform.

The timing had to be just right. Standing on the platform, Dan faked a cramp, doubled over, holding his side. Ian crossed the rope bridge and leaped onto the cargo net.

He started climbing faster once he saw that Dan wasn't moving.

Wait for it . . . wait . . .

When Ian was two-thirds of the way up the first section of cargo net, Dan dropped to his knees. He unhooked the second net from under the platform, scrunched the top of it so he could hold it in one hand, and then threw it as hard as he could into the air.

Ian yelled.

Dan yelled, too.

Two entirely different yells: one of panic, the other of triumph.

Ian was caught.

CHAPTER 13

Amy knew she was in trouble as soon as the Kabras got out of the car.

She and Dan had counted on Isabel being impeccably dressed and groomed as always, wearing her signature stiletto heels. The plan had been to draw Ian one way and Natalie another into the forest, where surely Isabel wouldn't follow them. Dan would stall Ian, Amy would stall Natalie, and then they would double back to confront Isabel on her own.

But Isabel was wearing hiking sneakers and running step for step with Natalie.

It would be two against one at the waterfall.

Having scouted out the area earlier, Amy gained a bigger lead on the Kabras when she left the path for a smaller trail through the forest. If Natalie had been on her own, Amy could have tried losing her. But Amy had to keep track of where Isabel was, which meant continuing on to the waterfall.

Amy ran over a little wooden bridge that crossed a stream. A few yards farther on, she reached the clearing at the bottom of the falls. The waterfall was hemmed in between two rock walls covered with ferns and other lush plant life. It spilled down over a series of rock shelves, almost like a steep staircase.

Amy splashed into the water and began climbing the rocks right into the falls. There were four shelves of rock that could be climbed. Amy scaled them quickly but carefully; they were slippery with moss and algae.

The fifth shelf was too high to reach. It formed the roof of a shallow little cave, with the water pouring down the front of it like a curtain. Already soaking wet, Amy clambered onto the fourth shelf and slipped through the waterfall.

It wasn't exactly a hiding place. One look at the falls, and anyone could guess where she had gone.

She took a few steps toward the back of the cave and found the gear she and Dan had left there earlier: a mosquito net and some rope. The plan had been that if she couldn't lose Natalie, she would lead her here, throw the net over her, and tie her up. It had been Dan's idea; after deciding to trap Ian in the cargo net, he must have had nets on the brain.

It wasn't a very good plan to start with; Amy was pretty doubtful about being able to get Natalie tied up. And now, with Isabel in the picture, too . . .

Amy's hands were shaking. What could she do against both of them? She looked around wildly, as if a solution might suddenly appear out of thin air.

Nothing. Her mind was blank, except for a feeling

of terror. Any second now, the murderer of her parents would burst through the curtain of water.

If Isabel hadn't been right next to her, Natalie didn't know if she would have recognized her mother. She was soaking wet—totally inelegant—and climbing the rocks faster than Natalie thought possible.

Isabel stepped through the waterfall with Natalie right behind her. Natalie watched as her mother tossed her head gently, to shake out some of the water in her hair. She was suddenly not in a hurry anymore.

Natalie saw Amy standing against the rock wall. Isabel stretched out her hand. "The dragon, please?" she said. Her voice was raised so she could be heard over the din of the waterfall; still, Natalie was impressed by her mother's utterly calm demeanor. It was as if she were asking Amy for a chocolate or something.

"I—I don't have it with me," Amy said, edging away from Isabel. "You can search me if you want. I'm telling you the truth. It's not here, I left it back in town."

"In that case, you're coming with us," Isabel said. "Where are your cohorts? Never mind, it doesn't matter. We'll get word to them somehow, and I'm sure that once they hear of the—well, the *plans* I have for you—they'll come running."

Natalie didn't know what her mother's plans were, but it wouldn't be lunch and shopping, that was for sure. She felt a little flutter in her stomach.

No blood. Please, no blood, it—it's so . . . disgusting.

Natalie immediately felt guilty for her disloyalty, but she still couldn't quell the thought.

Isabel stepped forward, grabbed Amy's arm, and dragged her through the curtain of water. She pushed Amy down the rock steps, her grip so tight that Amy cried out in pain. Natalie followed, almost losing her balance several times on the slippery surface.

"We're going back to town, and you will give me that dragon," Isabel said, as if nothing could be simpler. "Then we'll get in touch with that nanny of yours."

They made their way back onto the path. Amy was doing her best to struggle against her captor but without success. Isabel's grip was like iron.

The little wooden bridge came into view. Then—

"AMY! RUN!"

Natalie saw Amy react immediately. She backward-head-butted Isabel on the chin. Isabel shrieked in pain as Amy broke free of her grasp and ran over the bridge.

There was a sudden rattling sound; Natalie couldn't make out what it was. She and Isabel raced onto the bridge.

Too late, Natalie saw dozens of small round brown objects rolling around in front of her. She slipped on one and lost her balance. The same thing happened to Isabel. Natalie grabbed on to a bridge strut to stop her fall. Her mother was not so lucky.

Isabel fell and struck her head on an iron post. She crumpled to the ground, unconscious.

Natalie cried out. She saw blood coming from a gash on her mother's forehead.

Then she heard someone say, "Designer dog turds. I knew they'd come in handy."

Amy could hardly believe her eyes.

It was Nellie.

She had thrown dozens of nutmegs onto the bridge and now stood at the other end, waving an empty bag.

Just then Amy heard footsteps approaching.

"Amy?"

It was Dan. He came into view and stopped abruptly, taking in the scene in front of him.

"What's going on?" he asked.

Nellie crushed the bag and put one hand on her hip. "I'm off duty when *I* say so, not when someone else tells me," she said, staring pointedly at Amy.

Amy looked at Nellie, her eyes wide with surprise.

"Yes!" Dan pumped his fist once. "And Ian's trapped in the net—it'll take him ages to figure out a way to get down. Did you get the fang?"

Amy blinked. "Not yet," she said.

The trio walked onto the bridge. Isabel was lying on her back, her limbs splayed awkwardly. Amy could hardly think straight. It was so strange to see the invincible and terrifying Isabel on the ground like a doll tossed aside by a child.

"We could"—Dan's voice came out a hoarse croak—"we could make sure that—that she doesn't bother us anymore."

Amy looked at him in wonder. *How does he always seem to know what's in my head?*

"Um, I don't mean—" Dan stumbled over the words. "But if—if maybe there's something that would keep her—sort of, out of action? For like, a month?"

What could they do? Hit her on the head again—would that do it? Break a few bones? Some hard kicks to the stomach and hope for internal injuries?

It had only taken a few seconds for Amy to have those thoughts, but already she knew the truth.

"We can't," she whispered.

She didn't just mean physically. She meant that they couldn't take that kind of revenge on Isabel. They had already agreed that it was justice they were after. This was another chance to prove that they were different from the rest of the Madrigals.

Dan sighed loud enough for both of them, a sigh of both relief and regret.

Natalie was kneeling over Isabel. She had taken off her jacket and was pressing the arm of it against the wound on her mother's forehead. She looked up.

"She's bleeding. Please, can you help me?"

Amy had never seen Natalie like this before. Of course, she was soaking wet, which didn't help, but still, Amy could tell that every vestige of polish was gone. Natalie looked like a frightened five-year-old.

Nellie checked Isabel over quickly. "Her pulse and breathing are fine. But that gash may need stitches."

"Stitches? You mean . . . a scar?" Natalie asked, apparently horrified.

Nellie ignored her. "Are you doing the honors?" she asked Amy.

Amy hesitated for a moment. *She's not dead—it's not like touching a dead body,* she told herself. Still, it was unnerving to take Isabel's arm and push up her sleeve.

No bracelet on either arm.

"The fang," Amy said to Natalie, "where is it?"

Natalie pressed her lips together and shook her head.

"You want us to search her? We can do that," Nellie said with more than a little menace in her voice.

Amy glanced quickly at Natalie, then back at Nellie.

"Give me a minute?" Amy said. "You, too, Dan."

Dan looked indignant. But he and Nellie walked off the bridge and went to stand several yards away.

Amy knelt down next to Natalie. "I need that fang," she said. "If your mother starts to come to, we'll have to knock her out again, and that wouldn't be good for her. Tell me where it is and we'll help you get her to a doctor."

Natalie frowned but said nothing.

Amy pushed harder. "She might already have a concussion. The longer we sit here, the worse it is for her."

Natalie looked desperate. "A trade," she said. "You have a dragon she wants. I'll give you the fang, you give me the dragon."

Amy shook her head. "I can't do that," she said.

Long silence. Natalie took the pressure off her mother's wound; the bleeding had stopped. "She's going to hate having a scar," she whispered. "Do you think makeup will cover it up?"

Her mom is knocked out cold and bleeding, and she's talking about makeup??

But Natalie really did look worried.

"I don't know much about makeup," Amy said slowly. "My mom—she never got to show me. I was only seven when she died." Pause. "There are so many things I never got to do with her."

"Shopping," Natalie said. "That's what my mum and I do together mostly."

"Yeah," Amy said quietly. "I'll never get to go shopping with my mom."

Natalie's eyes widened. "That's just awful."

Amy leaned forward. "Natalie, please," she said. "Your mom needs to get to someone who can help her."

Natalie looked back at Isabel. "Promise?" she said, her voice quavery. "Promise you—you won't hurt her anymore if—if I—"

Amy raised her hand, Scout style. "I swear," she said.

Natalie reached for one of the interior pockets at the waistband of her mother's trousers. "She put it in here," she explained. "She said that if anything happened, she might have to take off her jacket, but it would take a lot more nerve for someone to take off her trousers."

"That's pretty smart," Amy said, and meant it.

Natalie lifted the Velcro-sealed flap of the pocket and took out the fang, which was on a key ring. "She found it ages ago," she said. "She usually wears it on her charm bracelet, but she said this was safer today." She handed it to Amy, who looked at it for a moment, then closed her hand around it tightly.

Amy stood up. "Just stay here," she said. "We'll call emergency, and someone will come help you."

Natalie furrowed her brow in thought. "Wait," she said. "Do you have anything you can tie me up with?"

"You want me to tie you up?" Amy asked, startled.

Natalie nodded. "When she wakes up and finds out the fang is gone—"

"Oh, I get it," Amy said. She gave Natalie a half grin.

"That's pretty smart," she said, and meant it again.

CHAPTER 14

Back in the car, Dan high-fived Amy so hard that her palm stung.

"We did it!" he yelled. "Cobras—go worm away on your bellies and crawl into a hole somewhere! Ha!"

Amy let herself enjoy the spark and fizz of his excitement for a few moments. Her own response was much more subdued. She felt almost dazed by the idea that they had actually gone after Isabel Kabra and succeeded in securing the fang.

Dan's enthusiasm bubbled over into a complete lack of caution. "Now we've got icons for all four branches!" he crowed, totally oblivious to Amy's look of dismay.

Great. Nellie only knew about the snakes and the fang before, but now she knows everything.

Dan babbled on. "But we still don't know what they're for, so what do we do next?"

Amy had thought this through already. "Nellie, will you call Miss Alice? Ask her if she remembers if there was anything that Grace was really interested in when she was here. I mean, something other than the earring."

The phone calls that followed proved even more productive than they'd hoped. Miss Alice recalled that Grace had been fascinated by the archaeological site of Port Royal and had spent a lot of time there. At Miss Alice's suggestion, they then phoned Lester at the Archives. Because Lester was a historian, he knew all about Port Royal. He would meet them there when he got off work.

The route to Port Royal took them onto the Palisadoes, a long spit of land that curved out into the ocean. The peninsula was so narrow that at times they could see the waters of Kingston Harbour on one side and the open sea on the other. Lester had instructed Nellie to drive to a church called St. Peter's. It was not a grand, impressive cathedral—just a small white church.

Lester was already there and greeted them with that nice smile of his.

"This is St. Peter's," he said. "There's something here I want you to see."

He led them to the churchyard, where there was a little cemetery.

"This one," he said, pointing to a tombstone that lay flat on the ground.

Amy read the inscription aloud.

"'Here lies the body of Lewis Galdy who departed this life at Port Royal on December 22, 1739 aged 80. He was born at Montpelier in France but left that country for his religion and came to settle in this island where he was swallowed up in the Great Earthquake in the year 1692 and by the providence of God was by another shock thrown into the sea and miraculously saved by swimming until a boat took him up. He lived many years after in great reputation. Beloved by all and much lamented at his Death.'"

"'Swallowed up in the Great Earthquake'?" Dan asked.

"June 7, 1692," Lester said. "A huge earthquake, followed by tidal waves and aftershocks. Supposedly, Lewis Galdy fell into a fissure like a lot of other folks. Most of them died when the aftershocks sealed the fissures. But somehow he got ejected and ended up miles out at sea."

"What a ride!" Dan exclaimed.

Lester grinned. "I thought you'd be interested."

"It's amazing he got through it alive!" Amy said.

"The earthquake destroyed two-thirds of the city," Lester said. "You probably noticed on the way here, it's pretty quiet now, just a small fishing village."

"That must have been one heck of an earthquake," Nellie said.

"I bet it was the waves," Dan said. "Like tsunamis. They probably swamped the place."

"Close," Lester said, "but not quite. The whole city was built on sand. The earthquake and the tidal waves destabilized the ground, and nearly the whole city got sucked down in quicksand."

Dan's mouth fell open. "A whole city? Wow!"

"It's called the Sunken City now, over that way," Lester said, pointing to the northeast. "I do some research for the excavation crew. The Sunken City is considered one of the richest archaeological sites in the Caribbean—in the whole Western Hemisphere, actually. A seventeenth-century city, preserved underwater!"

Amy found his enthusiasm contagious. She had always loved history, but Lester was making her realize that it wasn't just dates and places and names. The past was alive all around him, every day.

"There are also a number of ships that are important salvage sites," he said. "They're being carefully excavated, too."

Amy was paying close attention. "Can we go there? Can we see any of the excavation work?"

Grace, she thought. *Miss Alice said Grace spent a lot of time here. Probably poking around looking for stuff related to Anne Bonny or Nanny. A dig site would be the perfect place to start figuring out what she was looking for. . . .*

"You'd like to see it?" Lester's smile was even wider than usual. "They don't normally allow tourists, but I'll see what I can do," he said, and winked.

Dan beamed back at him. "Lester, you rock!"

Lester laughed. "Thanks. But reggae is more my style."

"Okay," Dan said cheerfully. "Lester, you reggae!"

In the car, as they neared the oceanfront on the other

side of the peninsula, Amy marveled for the hundredth time at the color of the sea.

"Az-tur-pea-lean," she whispered again.

Then she blinked.

Amy took the magnifying glass and the little gold strip out of her backpack.

"What?" Dan said. "Did we miss something?"

Amy's eyes were glowing. "I got it!" she said. "It's not words at all. It's sort of—it's like abbreviations." She scrabbled around in her pack again and took out a pen and her little notepad.

"Look," she said as she wrote.

EKTOMALUJA
EK – Ekaterina
TOMA – Tomas
LU – Lucian
JA – Janus

"Cool!" Dan said. "That's gotta be it!" Then his face fell. "But it's the same old problem. Even if we figured out what it says, we don't know what to do with it." He smacked one fist into the other palm in frustration. "It's so annoying!"

Amy put the strip of gold away again. "I know," she said, "but two steps forward, one step back—that's still progress."

Dan refused to be soothed. "NO steps back would be better," he muttered.

The Port Royal excavation site was an archaeological dig, not a tourist attraction. The work was mostly being done in a Quonset hut not far from the main pier.

Lester ushered them inside the hut. It was a single huge space. Long tables lined both side walls. Along the back wall were desks and computers. There were half a dozen people in the room, working at the tables or on the computers. Down the middle of the floor, there were crates full of mysterious objects and piles of stuff on top of and under tarps. It was impossible to tell what the "stuff" was; everything seemed to be encrusted with the same shade of brownish grayish green.

Amy felt a little thrill run through her. Those colors—rust and barnacles and algae—meant everything in those piles had come from beneath the surface of the ocean. From the Sunken City, or from ships . . .

"This project is to excavate five buildings that were buried in quicksand and have been remarkably well preserved," Lester said. "On the walls, you'll see architectural drawings of what the houses used to look like."

"Is any of the stuff here from pirate ships?" Amy asked.

"It's possible," Lester said. "The ships themselves, we're not working on those. That's being done by private salvage companies. But Port Royal was a pirate haven for many years. We might never know for sure, but the artifacts we're finding in these buildings—it's very likely that some of them were once in pirate hands."

Amy gave Dan a meaningful glance. Something Anne Bonny had touched could be in this very room.

"Go ahead and look around," Lester said. "Please don't touch anything, but I'll be happy to answer your questions. On this side"—he pointed to the left wall—"they're restoring the larger items and on the right, the smaller ones."

Amy and Dan headed for the right side of the hut. Three people were working at the long tables, using a variety of tools. Some looked like dentists' implements—delicate scrapers and picks. There were magnifying glasses and jewelers' loupes and even a microscope. There were all sizes of brushes, too, from the kind you would use to wash dishes to the finest of paintbrushes.

One woman was working on what looked like a large bowl. Another had a very dirty-looking set of silverware in front of her. Amy walked slowly down the length of the room, pausing now and then to watch the work. It was painstaking, she could tell; it probably took days to clean a single fork.

"We use mechanical methods of cleaning first," Lester explained, "meaning that we try to clean the objects by hand. If something really can't be cleaned that way, they'll use chemicals. But that's much riskier. When you can't tell for certain what something's made of, you don't know how it will react if you put it into a chemical bath. So that's a last resort, and they do that at the university. We only do mechanical cleaning here."

Amy made her way to the last two tables. One table held objects that had already been cleaned. Each one was encased in a plastic zipper bag with a numbered label. On the other table were objects that would need a chemical bath. They were still crusty.

Amy looked over the cleaned items. Most of them seemed to be broken bits of pottery. One bag held a ceramic jug missing several pieces. A fancy silver box was carved all over with squiggly designs. Two pewter plates looked almost undamaged. There were several glass bottles, a bunch of clay pipes, and at least a dozen spoons, too, each in its own bag.

Dan was now standing beside her. "I don't know how we'll ever find it," he said.

"Especially when we don't know what 'it' is."

He waved hopelessly at the piles in the middle of the room. Then his arm stopped in mid-wave.

"Wait," he said, "we don't know what it is, but we do know something about it. Maybe we should look for bears and wolves and snakes, things like that."

Amy stood very still for a moment. Dan's words had triggered a thought, and she moved her gaze from the spoons to the silver box.

It was carved everywhere, not just on the top but on the sides, too. The carvings seemed completely random. They weren't wolves or bears, of course—that would be too easy. They were just squiggles and loops with uncarved recesses here and there in no discernible pattern.

"Dan," she whispered. "That box—see the empty space along the side?"

Dan looked where she was pointing.

"Am I crazy—"

"Yes," Dan said immediately, "I've been telling you that for *years*."

But Amy didn't feel like joking around. "That uncarved space," she said slowly, "it's like a rectangle, but the corners are rounded. I think it's the exact size and shape of *this*." And she tapped the dragon medallion at the center of her necklace.

Dan looked back and forth between the necklace and the box. Then he closed his eyes for a moment. When he opened them again he said, "There was a carved box listed on that manifest," he said.

"There was?" Amy said, her voice pitched high in both amazement at his memory—yet again—and the hope that they were on to something.

"We need to get a closer look at it," Dan said.

He went to fetch Lester, who was chatting with Nellie. The three of them walked toward Amy.

"Sure," Lester was saying. "I can take it out of the bag for you, but I can't let you touch it."

He slid the box out of its plastic protection. It was the size and shape of half a shoe box. "Interesting that you should ask about this," he said. "It's the only piece here that wasn't actually excavated from the ruins."

"Then where'd it come from?" Amy asked.

"An anonymous donor," Lester said. "It came with a letter stating that the box was a family heirloom from Port Royal—a family that had survived the earthquake. The donor felt it should be displayed with the artifacts from the dig."

He gave it a very gentle shake, and they all heard a faint noise. "The letter also said that no one had ever been able to open it. There's something inside, but we might never find out what it is. We've tried x-raying it, but it's apparently lined with lead. And we wouldn't destroy an artifact like this to get at what's inside. Have you ever seen those Chinese puzzle boxes?"

"I have," Nellie said. "They're really cool."

"Right," Lester agreed. "They're usually made of wood, with sliding panels. There's no lock, but the box won't open unless you slide the panels in exactly the right order. This seems to be something like that, except it doesn't have any panels, and so far we haven't been able to figure it out."

He held up the box so they could see it on all sides.

Amy and Dan both began a thorough inspection. In less than five seconds, Dan glanced at Amy with his eyes blazing. She stepped toward him immediately.

On the opposite side of the box from the medallion-shaped space, the carvings meandered randomly. But there was another empty space that Amy knew on sight was what had caught Dan's eye. You would never have noticed it if you didn't know what you were looking for.

It was the exact size and shape of the bear claw.

And sure enough, on the third side of the box, they found two snake-shaped squiggles, and on the fourth, an elongated triangle the same size as the wolf fang.

"Excuse us," Amy mumbled, and dragged Dan away several steps.

"Anonymous donor, gimme a break," he whispered excitedly. "It was a Cahill for sure!"

"That's probably how the box is rigged," Amy said, just as excited. "Put all four icons in place and the box opens! That's gotta be it!"

"We have to get hold of that box," Dan said.

"But how?" Amy had already started thinking about this as soon as she saw the bear-claw shape. "Even if we could steal it, that would be a horrible thing to do to Lester. He might even lose his job!"

"Of course we don't want to steal it," Dan said, "but it might be our only option."

"Excuse me?"

Amy turned, startled. She hadn't noticed that Nellie was standing close enough to eavesdrop.

"You're not stealing anything," Nellie said. "Not from this place."

Amy clenched her fists. "This doesn't concern you," she said.

Nellie looked at her coolly. "We'll see about that," she said, and stalked off.

CHAPTER 15

"Lester, can I talk to you for a minute?"

Nellie approached the table. Lester was putting the box down carefully on top of its plastic bag.

"Sure," he said. "What's up?"

Nellie touched the snake nose ring. Everything was so complicated . . . how could she possibly explain it all to him? Where should she start?

At the beginning, of course. With Grace. Everything started with Grace.

"Grace was really interested in this project, wasn't she?" Nellie said.

"Oh, yah," Lester said with a smile. "She was interested in everything about old Jamaica. I remember the time she was here, when I was just a little kid. She'd ask my Granma about all the old stories, and Granma would tell her, and I'd sit there listening. It's probably what made me want to study history."

"Did she know you were working on the project?"

"Oh, sure. She's the one who got me the job. She found out that a university in the States was teaming up with the Jamaican Historical Society to excavate the site. She gave a big donation and"—another smile—"got me an interview to be a researcher here. So now I work full time at the Archives and do consulting work on the project."

Nellie nodded. Grace the mastermind at work again.

Lester frowned. "She used to check in with me from time to time, ask how the project was going, if we'd found anything interesting. I hadn't heard from her in a few months. I should have gotten in touch myself."

He looked sad. They were both quiet for a moment, remembering Grace.

Nellie touched his arm. "Lester, I think we know something about Grace that you might not," she said. "Grace was interested in this project for a specific reason. There was something she was hoping to find."

Lester looked at her curiously. "What, exactly?"

"This is going to sound crazy," Nellie said, "but we're not sure if she actually knew what she was looking for. All we know is, she had come across bits and pieces of it over the years. And she died before she could finish her search, so Amy and Dan are trying to finish it for her. And me, too."

Lester seemed a little bemused now, but not alarmed. "Okay, I'm still with you," he said.

Nellie took a deep breath. "It was really important to Grace," she said. "And also secret—she wanted as few people as possible to know about it. So what it comes down to is this: We need that box." She nodded toward the table. "We think that's what Grace was looking for. We need to take it with us"—she raised her hand to stop Lester from objecting—"but we want to make a deal."

She rushed on before Lester could say anything. "We think we have at least part of what's needed to open it. You let us take the box to see if we can open it. Then when we're done with it, we give it back to you with the secret of how to open it."

She locked eyes with him.

He has to say yes, he just has to. If not, the people she was working for would be extremely displeased.

And they were no fun when they were displeased.

Lester looked at the box on the table. Then he glanced toward the back of the hut, at one of his colleagues working on a computer. Probably his boss. He looked at the box again, and finally at Nellie.

She waited in silence for what felt like hours.

"Okay, here's *my* deal," he said at last. "Grace meant the world to me and Granma. Before you showed up, I'd have said there was nothing I wouldn't do for her."

He shook his head. "I'd have been wrong. I can't do it—I can't let you take it. Not just because I'd lose my job. But because it goes against every principle of good historianship. You think you have a good reason for taking it. So does every other person or group or government in the world who's ever taken artifacts away from where they belong."

"But we'd return it! I swear!"

Nellie crossed her fingers surreptitiously, praying that what she said was true.

"It's not that I don't trust you," Lester said. "Really, I don't even *know* you. The fact that you knew Grace, and they're her grandchildren—I wish that could be enough. But it's not. I'm sorry."

Nellie's heart sank to the pit of her stomach. They'd have to steal the box, and if they could manage to pull that off, then Lester, who had been so nice, would hate them, and Miss Alice would hate them, too. . . .

Lester was staring at her so hard he was almost glaring. She held his gaze, not daring to blink or breathe, hoping her expression didn't give away that she was already trying to figure out how to steal the box.

After a long moment, he seemed to make up his mind and eased off on the laser-beam stare.

"You can't take the box," he said flatly, "but *I* can. I can say I want to do some research on it, and they'll let me take it off the site. So here's how it goes down. Whatever you need to do with the box, you do it with me there. That's nonnegotiable."

Nellie flung her arms around his neck. Not like she had to force herself—he was, after all, very . . .

"Thanks a million, Lester! You won't regret it, I promise!"

Her ebullient response drew Dan and Amy over. Nellie gave them a thumbs-up.

"YESSSS!" Dan said, and made a valiant attempt to moonwalk.

Nellie raised her eyebrows at Amy, who was smiling at Lester. She caught Nellie's glance and shrugged in return.

Jeez, she's a tough nut, Nellie thought. *I might be making progress with Dan, but she's a different animal altogether. . . .*

Grinning sheepishly, Lester disentangled himself from Nellie's embrace. He picked up the box and put it back in its plastic bag.

"I'll go talk to the boss," he said. "I'll meet you guys outside."

Outside the hut, the weather was changing. The sun was an angry orange ball, fighting against a huge pile of purple clouds. The wind rustled the fronds of the palm trees with an ominous whispering sound.

Amy rubbed her bare arms. The air was warm and humid, but the wind had a cool edge to it.

"Feels like a storm coming," Nellie said.

But Amy couldn't keep her mind on the weather for long. She fingered the dragon medallion. "I'll have to cut it off," she said, saddened by the idea. *Maybe Grace was always an evil Madrigal,* she thought, *but I loved the necklace before I knew any of that.*

"We'll probably only need it to get the box open," Dan said. "After that, maybe you can have the necklace put back together."

"Um, that might be a problem," Nellie said. "To get Lester to give us the box, I told him we might be able to open it, and we'd give it back to him with the secret of how it opens."

"That's still okay," Dan said. "Telling him how to open it doesn't mean we have to give him all the stuff for it."

Amy looked dubious. "I don't know," she said. "What good is *knowing* how to open it if you can't actually open it?"

"Maybe they can have reproductions made of the medallion and the other stuff," Dan persisted.

Amy looked at him fondly. He understood how much Grace's necklace meant to her.

Just then, Lester came out of the hut. He was carrying a canvas-wrapped parcel.

The box. Amy felt a tingle of anticipation run down her spine.

"Okay, where should we do this?" Lester asked.

Amy thought for a moment. "Nellie, how about if we check in to a hotel? That would give us some . . . privacy."

"The Royal Harbour Hotel is right on the water," Lester said. "It's probably the nicest place in Port Royal, and it's just up the road."

"You guys walk," Nellie said. "I'll get the car and drive there with our bags."

The wind was getting stronger. It whipped Amy's hair into her eyes; she finally ended up holding it back with one hand.

They got to the hotel and waited just inside the entry. As Nellie pulled up a few minutes later, big slow blobs of rain began to fall. Amy and Dan rushed to help bring in the bags, including Saladin's carrier. He was making it very clear that he had not appreciated being left alone in the car. Dan took him out of the carrier and began petting him. Saladin gave a last huffy *mrrp,* but settled down in Dan's arms.

As Nellie checked in, Lester wandered over to the windows on the other side of the lobby. The view looked out toward the ocean, past a terraced restaurant that was roofed with palm fronds but otherwise open-air.

Amy went to join him. She peered out the window at the groups of diners in the restaurant. A few couples, a group of women, five people at a round table—

Amy gasped and turned pale.

Five people.

Ian, Natalie, two very large men—and Isabel.

Isabel Kabra, with a bandage on her head—a bigger version of the gauze Amy had worn two days earlier. Somehow, the bandage didn't make her look feeble or vulnerable; instead, like a pirate's eye patch or a motorcycle gang member's scar, it made her even more formidable.

Amy felt a flicker of what almost could have been admiration. Only a few hours earlier, Isabel had been unconscious and bleeding. She probably still had a whopper of a headache at the very least. But here she was doing all the talking as the group huddled together, clearly making plans.

And Amy knew for sure it wasn't a tea party they were planning.

"Dan!" Amy ran over to him. "The Kabras—they're here!"

"Where?"

Amy waved her hand frantically. "Out there. In the restaurant. They might come in here any minute now!"

"We have to warn Lester—"

As they hurried across the lobby to Lester, Amy wondered what to tell him. They could hardly give him a crash course in the Clue hunt—that would take hours. Just the most important thing, Amy decided.

"Lester," she said breathlessly, "there are some people in the restaurant, and if they come in here and see us—whatever you do, do *not* let them get anywhere near that box. They mustn't know anything about it—"

"They might try to steal it from you," Dan said. "Maybe you should pretend like you don't know us—"

Lester looked from face to face; Amy could tell he was completely befuddled.

"They're coming!" Dan said.

No time for a plan. "Look out the window," Amy said desperately. "That will put our backs to the room, and maybe they won't notice us."

Nellie was walking toward them. "All checked in," she called out. "What's going on?"

"It's the Kabras," Dan said. "We can't let them see Lester."

Nellie didn't ask any questions. She stood behind Lester as they arranged themselves in a little cluster by the window, with Lester and the precious box in the middle.

"Here they come," Dan said.

The Kabras entered the lobby, followed by the two men, who were wearing tracksuits and sunglasses. The men were huge, both well over six feet of solid muscle. They looked like they ate Dan-size children regularly for breakfast.

Amy pretended as hard as she could to be fascinated by something outside the window, which at the moment was the rain pelting down. As the Kabra group walked past on the other side of the lobby, she could see them for a few moments in her peripheral vision. Then they were out of sight, and she fought the urge to turn around and watch them by counting off the seconds.

Two . . . three . . . four . . . If they were staying at the hotel, they would have reached the elevator by now, and if not, they should be just about out the door. *Five . . . six . . . seven . . .*

Seven did not prove to be a lucky number.

CHAPTER 16

"There they are!" Isabel's voice rang out through the lobby. "Hugo, Anton, quick!"

Amy whirled around. The Kabra group had indeed reached the elevator; Ian and Natalie were already inside. The doors slid shut, leaving Isabel with the two men; the floor numbers began to light up, indicating that the elevator was in motion.

Nellie turned to Lester. "Run! And whatever you do, don't let them get that box. We'll stall them."

Lester seemed about to speak, but Isabel was already striding across the room with her companions in tow.

Dan was still holding Saladin. Suddenly, he thrust the cat out toward Isabel and the two men. "STAY BACK!" he yelled, brandishing the cat in front of him. "This cat is dangerous! He has, um—feline—feline spongiform halitosis! It can be fatal to humans!"

Saladin cooperated by swiping the air with his claws extended and hissing fiercely. It seemed that he did not appreciate being described as disease ridden, even if the disease didn't really exist.

Isabel broke stride, and the two men stumbled into her. She bumped her head on the shoulder of one of the men. Letting out a shriek of pain, she put her hand to her forehead and staggered.

It was a delay of only seconds, but it was enough.

"Please, Lester!" Amy begged. "Go!"

Lester shook his head in bafflement, then edged his way out the door to the restaurant. Moments later, Amy saw him out the window, running through the rain along the beach back toward the excavation hut.

Just then, the elevator doors opened. Natalie and Ian stepped out after their ride up a few floors and back down again.

Isabel shook her head, as if clearing her vision. "Typical!" she yelled. "Where have you two been? Hugo, Anton, you idiots, don't just stand there! Go after the man—he's carrying something—he went that way!" She pointed at the restaurant door.

Dan hurriedly deposited Saladin in his carrier. The hotel bellman standing nearby looked alarmed and gave the cat a respectful berth.

Then Dan followed Amy as she and Nellie dashed toward the door, with Hugo and Anton on their heels.

Hurricane. That was the word that popped into Nellie's head as soon as she set foot in the open-air restaurant. The rain seemed to be coming at her *horizontally.* Nellie had never seen a hurricane before, except on TV. If this wasn't a hurricane, she didn't ever want to be within a thousand miles of a real one.

She ran through the restaurant, where the staff was hurriedly locking things down. At the far end of the terrace were shallow stairs leading to the beach. With Amy and Dan beside her, Nellie took the stairs in a single jump. Within a few strides she was soaking wet.

"This way!" she heard Amy scream into the wind.

They turned to the right. Far down the beach, they could see a blur that was Lester struggling against the storm. The beach was quite wide because the tide was out, or at least it had been before the storm began. But each wave that crashed in was bigger than the one before it.

What was the best way to slow down Isabel's thugs? Nellie risked a quick glance over her shoulder.

"HEY!" she hollered.

Hugo and Anton were no longer behind them.

"They must have gone out the front!" Dan screamed. "They're going to try to head him off!"

"We have to get to him first!" Nellie screamed back.

They had to scream to be heard over the howling wind.

Nellie tried to think. With the rain pummeling down and the wind shrieking, she could hardly hear her own thoughts. *They'll be faster, running on the road instead of on the sand. Lester has a good head start. But when he gets to the hut, then what? They'll get there before us. . . .*

They raced down the beach. Lester was almost to the hut now.

"Come on!" Amy shouted, and pulled ahead.

Nellie had thought that she was already running as fast as she could, but seeing Amy's burst of speed made her find one of her own.

Up ahead, Lester stopped abruptly. Nellie knew what that meant: He had spotted either Hugo or Anton.

Sure enough, Lester reversed himself and began running back toward them.

Behind him, Nellie saw one of the thugs. Where was the other one?

A few seconds later, she had her answer. The second man emerged on the beach not far ahead of them. Now Lester was caught between the two men, who were rapidly closing in on him. He moved forward a few more yards and then, to Nellie's astonishment, he turned to his right and started running.

Toward the ocean.

"What's he doing?" Dan yelled.

Hugo and Anton thundered after Lester, the Cahill gang right behind them. Through the pelting rain, Nellie could now see what she hadn't earlier. Lester, still hugging the box to his chest, was running on a narrow spit of sand that rose a little higher than the rest of the seabed and stretched far out into the water. Maybe he was hoping that the thugs wouldn't follow him. Who runs out into the ocean during a hurricane?

The spit was so narrow that the three of them couldn't run side by side. Amy was in front. Water was splashing around Nellie's ankles, but everything was so wet that she couldn't tell if it was rain or waves.

Beyond Amy's shoulder, Nellie saw Lester make a flying leap. He landed and stumbled forward a few steps. Then he turned and looked behind him.

Hugo and Anton had been running one after the other, barely two paces apart. Suddenly, they both tripped and fell forward.

But what had they tripped on? Nellie couldn't see a rock or a piece of driftwood or anything—just sand, with water roiling and swirling over it. . . .

"STOP!" Lester screamed. "DON'T COME ANY FARTHER! IT'S QUICKSAND!"

Amy stopped so fast that Nellie ran into her, and Dan plowed into both of them. Somehow, grabbing on to each other, they managed to remain upright. All three of them gaped at the scene before them.

Hugo and Anton had tripped because their feet had been sucked in by the quicksand that Lester had jumped over. They had already sunk in up to their knees and were struggling violently, trying to pull their legs out of the mire.

"NELLIE!" Lester yelled. "CATCH!"

He tossed the canvas parcel to her, then shouted, "GO BACK! WAIT FOR ME AT THE HUT!"

Yeah, right, Nellie thought, *like we're going to leave you out here on your own.*

But she backed up, and so did Dan and Amy.

Lester took a step toward Hugo and Anton.

"Listen to me," he shouted. "I'm going to tell you how to get out. Stop struggling; you'll only get sucked in more. Lie back, like you're floating on your backs—"

Anton and Hugo responded with a string of swear words, some of which Nellie had never heard before. They were still trying to pull themselves out.

One of them had already sunk in as far as his waist, the other to his thighs.

"Lie back!" Lester yelled again. "Spread out your arms and kick your legs like you're swimming! It's your only chance!"

He took another cautious step forward. Nellie could see that he was being careful to avoid the edge of the quicksand pit.

Then Hugo—or maybe it was Anton—gave an enormous bellow, lunged forward, and grabbed Lester's leg. If he was trying to use Lester to pull himself out, his strategy failed miserably.

Instead, he pulled Lester in.

"LESTER!"

Dan, Amy, and Nellie all screamed his name at once.

The two thugs were both yelling and grappling with Lester, one grabbing his arm, the other clutching at his belt. Lester almost fell face-first into the quicksand but grabbed on to Anton—or maybe it was Hugo—and straightened himself out. Then he used his elbow to whack one thug squarely in the nose. The thug howled and clapped both hands to his face.

"If you idiots don't want to die, you better listen!" Lester shouted.

Dan felt a surge of admiration. Lester was shouting so he could be heard over the thug's howls, but there was no panic in his voice. Dan wondered if he could ever be that cool under fire.

Hugo and Anton looked at each other, then at Lester. Both of them stopped struggling. Dan noticed that the storm had eased up a little. It was still pouring, but the wind wasn't howling anymore.

"That's better," Lester said. "Now. No one ever really sinks completely into quicksand—that's a Hollywood myth. As long as you keep your arms out, you'll only sink in as far as your armpits. The real danger now is the tide coming in. If we don't get out soon, we could drown."

Dan saw both thugs' eyes widen in fear.

"You." Lester pointed up to the thug who had fallen in first and was now mired to his chest. "What's your name?"

"Anton," the thug replied.

"Okay, Anton. Start wiggling your feet and legs. DON'T PANIC. Little motions, like kicking. Don't try to pull them out. What you want to do is get your body as horizontal as possible."

On hearing this, Hugo, who had fallen in after Anton and was therefore only up to his waist, immediately began moving, too.

"NO," Lester said to him sternly. "One at a time. Too much movement will destabilize the sand and we'll sink even faster. Anton goes first, he's in deepest—"

"Screw that!" Hugo yelled. Although, of course, Dan couldn't see what Hugo's legs were doing; they must have been moving like crazy because just as Lester had predicted, all three of them began to sink faster.

"CUT IT OUT!" Anton screamed. "You heard him, I go first!" He reared back and punched Hugo in the nose—the same nose that Lester had elbowed earlier. Hugo roared out a curse and grabbed his nose again.

Dan took a step closer, then squatted down. "Lester," he said urgently, "what can we do?"

"Go find a pole or a flat piece of wood or something," Lester said. "If they listen to what I'm saying, we shouldn't need it, but just in case—" He was now up to his waist in the quicksand himself; even so, he gave Dan a cheerful wink.

Dan looked at Amy and Nellie. "You go," he said. "I'll stay here. Hurry!"

Amy and Nellie started running toward the beach.

"BE CAREFUL!" Dan yelled after them.

The Kabras were still onshore somewhere.

CHAPTER 17

With Hugo somewhat subdued, Anton must have been able to wiggle his feet and legs the way Lester had told him to, because Dan saw that his head and shoulders were leaning back, as if he were trying to lie on top of the sand. The waves were lapping at his neck and chin.

"Good, you're in position now," Lester said as calmly as if he were giving a tennis lesson. "Pretend like you're floating on your back—move your arms and legs like you're swimming."

Dan watched in amazement as the rest of Anton's body gradually emerged from the quicksand.

"Any minute now, you should be able to roll out," Lester said.

Sure enough, a few moments later, Anton "swam" onto firmer sand and rolled onto his stomach. He pushed himself up on his hands and knees and panted, looking so much like a giant breed of dog that Dan almost laughed.

"Your turn," Lester said to Hugo. "Start wiggling your feet and legs."

Hugo ignored him. "Get over here and pull me out!" he yelled at Anton.

"He can't pull you out," Lester said. "The suction's too strong. You'll have to do what he did to get out."

"Do like he says," Anton said.

"GIMME YOUR HAND!" Hugo bellowed.

Anton shrugged. Then he lay down on his stomach and put out his hand. Hugo grabbed it and Anton started pulling. Hugo struggled against the muck.

"NO!" Lester yelled. "You're churning up the sand—"

Instead of being pulled out, Hugo sank in further.

"LET GO!" Anton yelled. "You're pulling me in!"

Hugo responded by grabbing on to Anton's arm with *both* hands. Anton made a fist with his free hand. "Let go or I'll bash your nose again!" he threatened.

The quicksand was moving, sliding around and rippling as if it were a living thing. Now Hugo and Lester were both up to their armpits in the mire. Hugo was much taller than Lester; the waves were lapping at his chin. But they were washing over Lester's mouth.

Just then the crest of a bigger wave broke over them. Lester managed to hold his breath in time, but Hugo emerged coughing and spluttering.

"Okay, okay!" he choked out. "I'll do it your way!" He glared at Lester, then looked up at Anton. "Hold him so he don't get in my way."

Anton grabbed one of Lester's arms, although Dan could see it that it was totally unnecessary. Lester wasn't getting in anyone's way.

"Go on," Lester said. "Lean back, wiggle your feet." He held his breath as another wave washed over him.

Hugo was mired deeper than Anton had been, so it was taking him longer to get his body into position. Now Lester could only take a breath by stretching his head up between waves.

"Lester!" Dan shouted. "Forget about him—save yourself!"

He looked over his shoulder. Where were the girls?

Hugo finally rolled out of the quicksand.

"Let's blow," Anton said.

"Wait!" Dan cried out. "You're just gonna leave him? After he helped you?"

Hugo shrugged. "Whatcha want us to do, kid? He said it himself, we can't pull him out."

"That's what he said," Anton agreed.

They began splashing their way toward the beach, leaving Dan at the edge of the quicksand pit with Lester all but fully submerged.

Dan glanced around frantically. No sign of Amy or Nellie. He looked at Lester, who was leaning back, obviously wiggling his legs in the quicksand. Dan knew that Lester could get himself out—if he didn't run out of air.

He thought he'd have enough time. He didn't count on the waves getting bigger so fast.

Another wave crested, and Dan saw to his horror that Lester could no longer take a breath between waves; his head was completely underwater.

A tube, like a snorkel, Dan thought desperately. Some sort of tube he could stick in Lester's mouth that would clear the top of the waves so he could breathe . . .

Dan patted his pockets frantically. Nothing there.

Nothing anywhere except water that was getting deeper by the minute.

Lester was still leaning back, working his legs and feet toward the surface. But as Dan watched, Lester's eyes began bugging out. He was almost out of air.

Dan had never felt so helpless. If he grabbed Lester and tried to pull him out, it would only make things worse. Should he run back to try to find help?

No! I can't leave him here alone—I'm all he's got!

And in that moment, Dan knew what to do.

Dan dropped to his hands and knees in the water. It was getting hard to tell where the edges of the pit were; he just had to trust that the sand would stay firm beneath him.

He took a huge breath and puffed his cheeks out, leaning over so Lester could see him clearly.

Lester jerked his head in a nod. He understood what Dan was doing.

Dan plunged his face into the water. He found Lester's mouth with his own and exhaled all the air in his lungs. Then he surfaced and wiped away the water streaming into his eyes.

It worked! Between waves, he could see Lester *smiling*!

"YES!" Dan pumped his fist once. A few more breaths should give Lester enough time to get out. He inhaled, went under, and gave Lester a second breath.

This time Lester gave him a thumbs-up. Dan was ecstatic. He still couldn't see the lower half of Lester's body, but surely it wouldn't be much longer. . . .

Dan took in another lungful of air. He leaned over, ready to go beneath the surface again.

A huge wave crashed into him, sweeping him head over heels toward the beach.

Dan tried to get up and was knocked down by another wave. Finally, he staggered to his feet and whirled around frantically.

Where was Lester?

The spit of sand that led to the quicksand was now completely underwater. Dan had no idea if he had been swept straight in or to one side. He didn't know if the wave had carried him five feet or twenty-five.

Where was Lester?

Four minutes. The thought surfaced in Dan's mind, popping up from wherever it was buried. Four minutes without oxygen before brain damage set in. He had to find Lester in the next four minutes.

"DAN!"

It was Amy, running toward him from the beach, holding a short plank.

"Amy!" He splashed over to her and grabbed the plank.

"Where—"

"I don't know!" he said. "I was right there with him—and then a wave—and he's stuck in the quicksand—we've got to find him!"

Despite that garbled explanation, Amy didn't question him. "Let's go," she said. "You look to the right, I'll look to the left, and we'll both keep checking the middle."

The rain had stopped and the sky was clearing; there was even a sunset now, purple and orange and oblivious to their distress. They ran out into the waves. As he searched the water desperately, Dan realized that he had no idea what to do with the plank. If Lester was unconscious—if he couldn't get himself out of the pit, and they couldn't pull him out—

Dan shut that thought out of his mind.

How much time had passed? A minute? Two minutes? The water was up to his thighs now. Had it been that deep at the pit? Were they already out too far?

If only Lester would stick his arm up out of the water so they could see where he was. . . .

Dan gasped as fear hit his stomach so hard he felt like he'd been punched.

Lester would have thought of that.

If he could raise his arm, he would have done it by now.

CHAPTER 18

Dan had heard of people being "in shock" before. He thought it meant like being really stunned so you couldn't talk or even get your breath.

This was different. He was breathing in tiny shallow gasps, trembling all over. His skin was cold and clammy; he felt cold inside, too. He had heard the ambulance attendant say it to Amy and Nellie. "He's in shock. We'll take care of him."

How long had it been? Since Amy had left him in the water to run and call for help; since she'd come back; since he had heard the wail of sirens, and the beach had filled up with people—police and ambulance and rescue, people milling around everywhere, and none of them mattered to Dan. Only one person mattered.

Lester.

They'd had to drag Dan out of the water. He was okay, he kept telling everyone, he was fine, it was Lester who was in trouble, he had to find Lester.

They had brought Lester up onto the beach, and Dan was still okay then; he had knelt next to Lester while the EMTs worked on him for what seemed like hours. A police officer wanted to interview him; he refused to budge from Lester's side, but he told the officer what had happened, beginning with Hugo and Anton chasing Lester out into the ocean, and how Lester had helped them escape from the quicksand. The police officer had been very gentle with him, not asking any hard questions, so Dan didn't have to explain *why* the two thugs had been chasing Lester in the first place.

Finally, they had taken Lester away on a stretcher. And even then Dan might have been okay, but as one of the EMTs closed the ambulance's bay doors, she looked at the police officer standing nearby and shook her head, and Dan could see it in her eyes, could see beyond any doubt, that there was no hope for Lester.

That was when he had gone into shock. Amy had been by his side, she had caught him as he fell to his knees, and then another EMT made him lie on a stretcher and put blankets on top of him, but still he couldn't get warm, and now that was all he could think about, how cold he was, shivering, shaking, his teeth chattering, cold to the very middle of his bones.

So cold that he'd never ever ever be able to feel warm again.

The hospital was keeping Dan overnight "for observation." A nurse came into the room from time to time, but she didn't need to do much observing. Amy was doing it for her.

She hadn't left Dan's side for hours. When the EMTs had put him in the ambulance, they had tried to explain that minors weren't allowed to ride along, but Amy had spoken to them so firmly that Nellie looked at her in surprise.

"I'm his only relative here, and she's our guardian," Amy had said, pointing at Nellie. "She's giving me permission to ride with him." And without waiting for a response, she had climbed into the ambulance.

Dan hadn't said a word since going into shock. He had looked at her just once, with so much bewilderment and grief in his expression that her eyes had instantly filled with tears. Finally, he had fallen asleep, and Nellie had made her sit in an armchair in the corner of the room with stern instructions to get some rest. Then Nellie had left to go talk to Miss Alice.

Poor Miss Alice . . . Amy could hardly bear to think of her. She was so old . . . would she survive the shock of hearing the news?

Amy woke an hour or so later. Before her eyes were even fully open, she was stumbling to Dan's bedside again. Nellie was right beside her.

As if sensing their presence, Dan stirred. Amy waited until he sat up a little, then poured him a drink.

Nellie reported that Miss Alice's niece was driving down from Montego Bay to be with her, and that Miss

Alice appeared to be bearing the news with considerable strength.

"She's pretty tough," Nellie said, admiration in her voice.

With a start, Amy remembered something. "Where's the box?" she asked. It was ages since she had last thought about it. "We split up on the beach," she explained to Dan. "Nellie had the box."

"Don't worry, it's safe," Nellie said, waving her hand as if brushing off the question.

Amy frowned. "Where?"

"I said it's safe," Nellie replied.

"But why won't you say where?"

"Can't you trust me for once—"

"Stop it! Just stop it!" Dan's voice was anguished. Stunned, both girls stared at him. Amy saw that he was clutching the bedsheet in both hands, so tightly that his knuckles were white. "I don't care about the stupid box anymore," he said, his voice cracking with strain. "Lester's *dead.* He died because of that box. If it were here, I'd smash it into a million pieces."

Tears began streaming down his cheeks. "I'd give up the box, and every clue, and the million dollars, too," he whispered, "if it would bring Lester back."

Amy had never seen him so miserable. She got up from her chair and sat on the bed next to him. Gently, she pried one of his hands loose from the sheet and took it in hers.

For what felt like a long time, the room was quiet except for the sound of Dan's sniffles. Amy waited until his tears stopped. With her free hand, she gave him a tissue from a box on the nightstand. She restrained her impulse to wipe his nose for him; she was pretty sure he wouldn't like that.

Dan wiped his eyes first. Then he blew his nose. It sounded exactly like a goose honking.

A tiny giggle escaped from Nellie; she immediately looked contrite and pretended to clear her throat.

Dan blew his nose again. This time, it sounded like a goose honking while being tortured.

Nellie burst out laughing, and Amy would have been appalled except that she found herself laughing, too. For a brief moment, Dan looked indignant, and then he was laughing hardest of all.

It was one of those things that none of them could have explained, the way they were laughing. They would calm down, then one of them would look at the other two and the giggles would start up and grow until they were laughing flat out once more. They laughed so hard that Dan's eyes began streaming again, and he had to blow his nose again, which produced the tortured-goose honk again, and of course made them laugh even harder. Amy put her hands over her mouth, trying in vain to stem the tide, while Nellie grabbed a pillow and buried her face in it.

At last their laughter faded into giggles, then silence. Amy's stomach muscles actually felt sore from all the laughing.

Just then the night nurse came in. She refilled Dan's water pitcher and plumped his pillows. "Time to go," she said.

"Thanks," Amy said. The nurse had let them stay way past visiting hours. Amy and Nellie had already decided that Dan would be safe in the hospital for one night. What with everything that had happened, they were sure that the Kabras would be lying low for at least a little while. The girls would go back to the hotel and come get Dan in the morning.

They said their good-nights. At the door, Amy turned and went back to the bed.

Dan already looked half asleep. She leaned over and gave him a quick kiss on his forehead.

It had been a long time since she'd given him a kiss. He didn't really respond, just wriggled deeper under the sheets and closed his eyes, which meant, she knew, that he didn't mind.

CHAPTER 19

"It's not like with Irina."

From the backseat of the car, Dan's voice was barely above a whisper.

The doctor who had signed off on Dan's chart that morning said there was nothing physically wrong with him, but that he might feel a little woozy from the sedative given to him in the night. "Good food, sunshine, relaxation, that's my prescription," the doctor declared.

No, Amy had thought. *That won't do it. What Dan needs is to rewind everything, back to a time when Lester was still alive.*

Looking at her brother's pale, exhausted face, Amy knew exactly what he meant about Irina.

Irina had *chosen* to be part of the Clue hunt. She had known about both the rewards and the risks and had made the deliberate decision to participate despite the potential dangers. She had died in full knowledge that her death was a consequence of the battle over the Clues.

Lester hadn't known any of that.

"It's so unfair," Dan said. "All he wanted to do was be helpful." Tears slid out from behind his closed eyelids. "And we never gave him a chance."

Tears were rolling down Amy's cheeks, too, but now she cleared her throat. "What do you mean?" she asked.

Dan opened his eyes. "We should have told him. That it might be dangerous to help us. We should have given him a chance to decide."

He used his T-shirt to wipe his eyes. "We're Madrigals, all right. I mean, we knew that before, but we were thinking we could be different, right? This proves we can't. Lester died, and it was our fault."

"But—but we didn't set out to—to kill him. Or anyone! Not even close!"

Dan shook his head. "It doesn't matter. Whether we meant to or not, that doesn't change anything for Lester."

Amy's insides twisted. The pain in Dan's eyes mirrored the pain in her own heart—to the nth degree.

It was too much to bear.

Amy almost choked on the lump in her throat. She had to try twice before she could speak. "Are you thinking what I'm thinking?" she whispered.

He nodded. "Yeah," he said.

She didn't have to stop to consider it. "Okay."

"Okay," he echoed.

There was no need for more words.

"Airport."

Nellie slammed on the brakes. Fortunately, they weren't even out of the parking lot yet.

"Airport? What for?" she demanded.

Amy was staring out the window. "We're going home," she said hoarsely. "Back to Aunt Beatrice."

"WHAT?!"

"It's the only way," Dan said. "We're Madrigals. Madrigals hurt people. Even kill them, or at least get them killed. We have to get out of the hunt before it happens again."

The silence that followed lasted for several moments.

"You sure about this?" Nellie said at last.

"Yes." They spoke in one voice, quietly but without hesitation.

Nellie drove onto the road.

Dan stared out the car window. *My last views of Jamaica . . . I'm* never *coming back here again.*

Then a guilty thought occurred to him.

We should go see Miss Alice. He was about to mention it when he saw the sign for the airport exit whiz by.

"Hey, that was the turnoff for the airport," he said. "You missed it. But it's okay—I was thinking we should go see Miss Alice before we leave."

Amy looked at him sadly. "You're right," she said.

"So, Spanish Town instead of the airport," Dan said, wondering what he could possibly say to Miss Alice.

No reply from Nellie.

And she wasn't wearing her earbuds.

"Nellie?" Amy said. "We want to go see Miss Alice, did you get that?"

Nellie pulled her sunglasses off the top of her head and put them on. "I heard you," she said. "Just sit back and relax. You could both use some rest."

"But this isn't the right way," Dan said. "Spanish Town is that way—" He jerked a thumb over his shoulder, indicating the opposite direction.

After another moment or two, it became clear that Nellie had no intention of turning around, and Dan felt his confusion turning into a vague sense of dread.

"Where's Lester's box?" he said suddenly.

"I told you, it's safe," Nellie replied.

He could see Nellie's reflection in the rearview mirror. She gave him a thin little smile.

"Don't worry about it," she said. "Remember, the doctor said you should take it easy."

"I'll take it easy as soon as you tell me where the box is," Dan said.

Nellie's lips tightened. Then she said, "I'm not answering any more questions. You'll understand everything once we get there."

"Get WHERE?" Dan's voice rose. "Where are you taking us?"

No answer.

Amy must have felt the same panic he did, because now she grabbed the door handle.

"Stop the car," she said. "I'm getting out—I'm not going any farther until you tell us what's going on."

"Sorry," Nellie said. "This is an express car. No stops until—the terminus."

The terminus. The way she said it sounded ominous to Dan.

Amy jerked the door handle. The child latch was engaged; they were locked in.

"For your own protection," Nellie said.

For a wild moment, Dan thought of grabbing the steering wheel or putting his hands over Nellie's eyes—anything to make her stop. But there were other cars on the road; someone else might get hurt.

Dan's heart was pounding so hard that he could feel his pulse in his throat. He tried to speak, but no words came out. He could only stare in disbelief at the back of Nellie's head.

All this time she was helping us just so we would let our guard down.

And we did, and now she's sucker punched us.

After a few minutes on the road, Nellie pulled over and made a call on her cell phone.

"On my way," she said. Then, "No. Didn't work out. But they're with me. Which means Plan B."

The words were both cryptic and frightening, but to

Amy, the scariest thing of all was the flatness of Nellie's voice. She could have been a robot; there was not a shred of emotion in her words. And her face looked as cold as stone.

Kidnapped. We're being kidnapped.

Amy didn't even try to ask what Plan B meant; she knew she'd get no answer. With trembling fingers, she undid her seat belt and climbed into the backseat. She needed to be near Dan.

Amy wanted to feel furious at this final, incontrovertible evidence of Nellie's betrayal. Instead, she was almost overwhelmed by a wave of exhaustion.

I'm so tired. Too tired and sad to be angry. She wished she could curl up into a ball in a dark, soundless room and sleep and sleep and sleep. For, like, ten years.

Turning her face toward the window, Amy closed her eyes helplessly. A few tears wet her lashes.

After they had driven about an hour and a half—in utter silence—Nellie turned the car off the highway onto a smaller road that wound through the mountains. Although the mountains seemed to be almost pure wilderness, they did pass an occasional house. A few houses close together made up a town. The road grew narrower and steeper at every turn and finally brought them to an iron bridge paved with steel plates that crossed a gully.

MOORE TOWN the sign on the bridge read.

Nellie drove across the bridge and stopped the car on the other side. She popped the door locks.

"You can get out," she said in that same expressionless voice. "But don't even think of running anywhere."

She can't stop both of us, Amy thought. *Maybe I could distract her and Dan could make a run for it. . . .*

Amy got out of the car and looked around. Moore Town wasn't like any town she had ever seen before. The houses hopscotched to either side of a dirt track that led up the mountainside. Some were painted in tropical colors—blue, pink, lemon yellow—faded but still cheerful. The mountains beyond were draped in a blue-gray mist that blurred their edges.

Dan walked around the car and stood next to her. "What now?" he asked anxiously.

"That's up to you."

The voice had come from behind them. Soft, raspy . . . As Amy turned around, she grabbed Dan's hand, knowing exactly who she would see.

The man in black.

Who was dressed all in gray now.

Amy stood paralyzed. She saw that he was holding a familiar canvas-wrapped parcel.

The box.

Nellie had given it to the man in black.

CHAPTER 20

"NOOOOO!"

Dan wrenched his hand out of Amy's and launched himself forward. His rage was palpable. Amy knew there was no way he was going to allow the box—Lester's box—to remain in the hands of the enemy.

For an old guy, the man proved surprisingly agile. He sidestepped Dan's charge and thrust out his foot. Dan tripped and ended up sprawled in the dirt.

Amy rushed to his side.

He looked up at her wildly. "We can take them—you go for Nellie and I'll—"

"Oh, please," the man in gray said. "And then what—run to escape us? Exactly where do you plan on running to?"

In desperation, Amy realized he was right. He had probably chosen this location for exactly that reason. It was miles away from anywhere safe, and Dan was surely still too weak to run very far.

"Perhaps you should hear me out instead," the man

said. "Shall we go somewhere more comfortable where we can talk?"

"You tried to kill us!" Dan shouted. "In Austria! Why would we ever sit down with a *murderer*?"

The man looked surprised. "You have misunderstood. Forgivable, given that you do not have all the facts. I'm afraid I must insist on our sitting down together. I am alone at the moment, but I have help nearby." He held up a cell phone. "I assume you would rather talk to me than to some of my less genteel colleagues."

The threat could not have been any clearer.

They sat under an awning at the side of one of the buildings, a combination bar and general store. Nellie took the box and locked it in the car. Then, oddly, she did not sit down with them but went to stand by the side of the road.

Amy and Dan sat next to each other, opposite their adversary.

"Do you know about Moore Town?" the man asked.

Amy had already decided not to say one word more than necessary to him. Neither she nor Dan replied. It was apparently a rhetorical question anyway; the man continued speaking, unfazed by their lack of response.

"It was one of the original settlements of the Windward Maroons," he said. "Another was Nanny

Town, named, of course, for The Right Excellent Nanny."

Amy shivered. It seemed that he already knew about their Nanny investigations. *Of course. Nellie must have told him.*

Nellie must have told him everything.

"It was both her home and her base of operations," he continued. "I wish Nanny Town could have been our meeting place, but it's been abandoned for many years now."

He took a sip of his drink. "The bridge you crossed over is the only access to the town," he said. "The Maroons were very clever; all of their settlements had only one point of entry. It made the towns easy to guard. Just a few Maroons could hold off much larger numbers of British troops. Nanny Town had a similar defense; it was on a high spur overlooking a river."

Amy glanced at Nellie, whose back was to them. Nellie seemed to be watching the road back toward the bridge.

The man followed her gaze. "Yes, that's right," he said. "She's standing guard. With her there, no one can sneak up on us, because the only way into Moore Town is along that road."

"Not interested in a geography lesson from someone who tried to kill us," Dan snapped.

That was the only good thing about the mess they were in: Dan's anger had made him much more himself.

The man inclined his head. "But of course. Your impatience is understandable."

He interlaced his fingers and put his hands on the table in front of him.

"The first thing I should tell you is that I am speaking to you on behalf of the Madrigals."

Amy nudged Dan under the table. She could feel his anger seething. *Stay calm,* she tried to tell him telepathically. *Focus. We have to find a way to get that box back and then get out of here. . . .*

"The Madrigals have been following your progress with great interest," the man said. "They are quite impressed. I have been charged with the task of discovering how you perform on a particular task they have set for you."

"We're not doing anything for them!" Amy burst out.

The man shrugged. "Fine. But I must tell you the consequences for not cooperating. Without going into too much detail, you should know that we are holding your other companion."

"Our other—?" Amy stopped, aghast.

Saladin! She had been so exhausted at the hotel the night before, she hadn't even noticed that the cat wasn't there.

"You—you better not—you just leave him alone!" Dan could barely get the words out.

"Wh-what have you done to him?" Amy's voice quavered. She didn't even want to imagine what they might do to Saladin. . . . Who were these people who would threaten a poor innocent cat?

"Why, nothing," the man said. "He's perfectly fine. And will continue to be, so long as you cooperate. It's quite simple: All you have to do is get the box to open."

"I want your word on something," Dan said. Amy could tell from his voice that he was still struggling to suppress his fury.

"You're hardly in a position to negotiate."

"You're wrong about that. You want us to do this. If you didn't, you'd just do it yourselves. So I want something in return."

The man said nothing.

Dan went on. "Once you get your precious little secret out of the box, I want it back. The box—and Saladin."

The man shrugged. "I believe that can be arranged."

"I want your word on it," Dan said doggedly. He looked at the man with an expression of disdain. "That is, if your word is any good," he added spitefully.

The man winced, then held up his hand.

"You have my word," he said with a bow of his head. When he glanced up at Dan, Amy was startled to see a look of—could it be respect? Or maybe even pride?—in his eyes. Only for the merest second, though; maybe she had imagined it.

"If you're finished," she said coldly, "we'd like to get started."

"Miss Gomez?"

Nellie trotted back from her sentry position.

Like his lapdog, Amy thought in disgust.

But beneath that disdainful thought, she could still feel a deep ocean of sorrow over Nellie's betrayal.

"Please retrieve the box," he said, "and then you and I will be leaving these two in peace to attempt the completion of their task."

"What?" Nellie frowned.

"I believe you heard me quite clearly."

"No!" Nellie shouted. "That was not part of the deal—you said I could help them!"

Amy's heart leaped in her chest. *Could Nellie be—a* triple-*crosser?* Amy tried to quash the thought; she couldn't bear to get her hopes up only to have them crushed again.

"The deal, Miss Gomez, is whatever we say it is."

Nellie narrowed her eyes. "You think?" She ran to the car, opened the door, and held up the keys.

"If you don't let me help them," she yelled, "I'll drive off right this minute. With the box."

The man in gray seemed unperturbed. "How long do you think it would take us to track you down?"

"Long enough for me to give the box to the Kabras," she shot back.

A flicker of unease crossed the man's face, but in the

next moment he was back in control. "Now, now," he said. "No need to be hasty about this."

"I mean it!" she yelled. "Just try me!"

The man held up his hands. "Calm down, please," he said, then shrugged. "You may remain with them if that is your desire."

"You got that right," Nellie muttered. She stalked back to the table.

Amy stared at her.

What's going on?

One way or another, they were about to find out.

Nellie removed her nose ring and got out Miss Alice's matching snake. Amy put her dragon necklace and the wolf fang side by side in front of her. Dan took the bear claw off its chain.

"You'll need these," the man said, and produced a small pair of pliers.

Nellie used them to snip the post off her nose ring and Miss Alice's earring. She passed the pliers to Dan, who clipped the hanging bail from the claw.

Amy took up the pliers. She hesitated for only a moment before cutting the dragon medallion free from Grace's necklace.

The man unwrapped the carved box and handed it to Nellie. She fitted the snakes into place on one side.

Dan did the same with the bear claw.

Then Amy put the fang on the third side of the box. She picked up the dragon medallion and held her breath.

The dragon snapped into place neatly.

The box did not open. Amy let out her breath. *Of course not,* she thought. *It's not* magic, *for heaven's sake.*

She tried opening it the way you would a normal box.

No luck.

"Here, let me try," Dan said eagerly. He worked his way around all four sides trying to open it; he even turned it upside down.

Still no good.

The man in gray was watching them, leaning back in his chair a little with his arms crossed. He had donned sunglasses; Amy couldn't see his expression.

Nellie took a turn, too. For the moment, Amy had decided to stop wondering whose side Nellie was on; right now she and Dan needed all the help they could get.

They went around one more time. Amy tried opening the side panels, then sliding the top instead of lifting it.

Nothing.

The man in gray stood. "It appears that you have failed," he said, and reached for the box.

Dan snatched it up and put it behind his back. He glared at the man so ferociously that Amy almost shivered. She'd never seen him look like that before; she didn't know what would happen if the man tried to take the box away from Dan.

"Please," she said in desperation, "can't we have just a little more time? We have the icons, they all fit, we just have to figure out . . ." Her voice trailed off.

The man walked away a few steps. He took out a cell phone, dialed a number, and spoke quickly. Then he turned and looked at them.

"It is now five minutes past twelve," he announced. "You have exactly one hour. If the box is not open by one-oh-five, you will have failed. Is that understood?"

Amy nodded.

"Young man?"

Dan was still glaring, but he nodded, too.

"I will be back in"—the man glanced at his watch—"fifty-nine minutes." He paused. "Remember, all sides of this are really one, and you need us to succeed."

The man walked away, leaving them with the box.

Forty minutes later, Nellie looked at Amy helplessly. Amy was near tears, and nothing Nellie could say would comfort her.

They had tried everything. They had taken the icons out and put them back in again, in every possible order. They had put all four icons in at the same time. They had stood the box on each of its four sides; they'd tried having two people push on different parts of the box at the same time. They had tapped and poked and prodded every square centimeter of it.

Nothing worked.

Amy's head was bowed in a vain attempt to hide her weeping. Sweat was running down Dan's face as he examined the box yet again.

Nellie felt like her head was about to burst. There had to be some way she could help. . . .

"Think!" she said. "We must have forgotten something. Think back to the very start—to the Bahamas."

Amy lifted her head a little. "The bear claw," she said. "That was the Bahamas."

Dan stopped fiddling with the box and looked up, too. "After that we came here—to Jamaica—and we found Miss Alice's snake."

Clearly, it was making them feel a little better to focus on something other than the box. "Then what?" Nellie encouraged them.

"Then you called your dad," Amy said, "and—"

"THE RIGHT EXCELLENT NANNY!" Dan shouted. "The gold strip from the horn!"

Amy was already digging into her backpack. She took out the little piece of metal, which had been carefully wrapped in a piece of paper.

Nellie saw her frown almost immediately.

"It doesn't fit," Amy said. "Look. It's longer than any of the sides."

"What about diagonally?" Dan suggested.

"Still too long."

"Maybe it's supposed to be bent," Nellie said.

"But how?" Amy asked.

Nellie's heart sank. Amy was right; there were probably about a million ways the strip could be bent. They'd never figure it out in time.

"This has to be it, this HAS to be it," Dan kept saying.

"Let me see it," Nellie said. "The strip, I mean."

She inspected it closely. Those tiny letters . . .

ektomaluja ektomaluja ektomaluja ektomaluja

"Why would it have lettering on both sides?" she asked. "I mean, if it fits into the box like the other pieces, there should be a 'right side' and a 'wrong side.' But there isn't. Both sides are the same."

Dan and Amy bent over the strip in Nellie's hand. Then Amy gasped. She dived into her backpack again and took out her notepad.

"I thought about this once before and then I forgot about it," she said. "Look."

She showed them the page where she'd written down the mystery word:

EKTOMALUJA
EK – Ekaterina
TOMA – Tomas
LU – Lucian
JA – Janus

"I wondered why Tomas got four letters when all the others had only two," she said. "It's because it's not T-O-M-A for Tomas." She scribbled furiously, then showed them the page again.

EK – Ekaterina
TO – Tomas
MA - MADRIGAL
LU – Lucian
JA – Janus

"Brilliant!" Dan shouted.

Nellie closed her eyes in concentration. "Remember what he said when he left? Something about how we needed them to succeed. The Madrigals."

"The four branches, one icon on each side of the box," Amy said. "Madrigals, in the middle of the code word . . . Madrigals in the middle somehow . . ."

Dan was frowning fiercely. He looked at Nellie. "What did you say before? You said something—I'm trying to remember—"

"About the man in black? I mean, gray?"

"No. Before that."

Nellie thought for a moment. "Oh, I remember. I was asking why the letters are on both sides."

She saw Dan go very still; she could almost hear the effort his brain was making.

"The lettering is *raised,*" he said, "and on both sides.

That means the letters fit—somewhere we can't see. Give me that strip."

Nellie watched as Dan fashioned the strip into a circle by joining the ends.

"See?" he said. "It could go like this, edgewise, not flat, and if you put it in exactly the right place—"

The three of them nearly cracked heads as they bent to examine the box again.

"It has to be the top," Amy said excitedly. "It's not any one of the four sides, so the top is like the middle."

It was Dan who found it: a narrow slit in the carvings on the top of the box. The slit was shaped like a loop, a rough oval into which the strip would fit.

Except that it didn't. The strip *almost* fit, but not quite. No matter how they positioned it, shifting it a tiny bit at a time, it wouldn't slide into the slit.

Nellie let out a moan of frustration. She took out her cell phone to check the time.

"It's one-oh-two," she said urgently. "He'll be back any minute now."

"There was something else," Amy said suddenly. "He said something else before he left. Besides the part about us needing the Madrigals."

"He said"—Dan narrowed his eyes in concentration—"he said to remember that all sides are really one."

"All sides are one," Amy whispered. "All sides are one. . . ."

There was a moment of complete silence.

Then Amy smiled. It was, Nellie thought, a *radiant* smile—there was no other word for it.

"Möbius strip," she said.

"What kind of trip?" Dan said.

"Not trip, *strip*," she said. "Möbius strip. It's a geometric shape that has only one side."

She took up the piece of gold and formed it into a loop again. But before joining the ends, she put a half twist into it. It now formed a wobbly ovalish shape.

"Look," she said. "If I were to put my pencil point here and trace a line down the middle of the strip, I could go all the way around until I came right back to where I started. And the line would show up on both sides, without me ever lifting my pencil. Which proves that it really has only *one* side."

"I don't get it," Nellie said.

"I'll show you again later," Amy said. "It works better with a strip of paper."

"FORGET IT!" Dan said. "Just see if it fits that way!"

"Okay, okay," Amy said.

Nellie could tell that Amy wasn't in any hurry now. She looked utterly calm and supremely confident.

Holding the strip in its Möbius shape, Amy inserted it into the slit. She tried once, twice, three times.

On the fourth try, the strip clicked perfectly into place.

There was a small pinging sound, and the lid of the box sprang open.

CHAPTER 21

"We open it together," Amy said, her eyes gleaming. "Ready? One—two—three—"

Inside, the box was lined with silk decorated with an elaborately embroidered whale. Two objects rested on the silk: a small roll of parchment and a little pouch.

Amy unrolled the parchment carefully. The edges crackled; a few tiny pieces flaked off. The ink on the page was faded but still legible. Amy read aloud:

The web of our life is of a mingled yarn,
Good and ill together.
Torn apart by years of greed,
now tatter, shred, and tangle.
So, like the spider, begin anew,
one web with many a tether.
Our silk tho fine as strong as steel!
From united threads we danngle.
MC In the year of our Lord 1548

"Can I see it?" Dan took the parchment gently from Amy's hands. He glanced at it quickly.

"WOO-HOO!" he whooped. "Finally, an easy one!"

With one hand, he made a beckoning motion with his fingers. "Go on, go on, ask me," he said.

Amy and Nellie rolled their eyes at each other.

"Okay," Nellie said, "whatcha got?"

Dan's expression was pure smugness. "I want you to beg," he said.

"Dan!" Amy said, half laughing but completely annoyed.

"Just kidding," he said. He held out the page and pointed to it. "See that? The word 'danngle.' It's misspelled. And it has to be, because without the extra 'n,' it wouldn't be an anagram for ENGLAND. That's where we go next!"

He mimed licking his finger and then touched his temple. *"Sssss,"* he said. "Oh, *yeah,* I'm good. I'm *so* good."

More eye-rolling from the girls. In an effort to distract Dan's attention away from his self-proclaimed greatness, Amy reached for the little pouch. It was beautifully made, lined and heavily padded and closed with a drawstring. She opened it carefully and took out a small glass vial.

The vial was filled with a rusty brownish red substance, like a rough powder. Amy uncorked the vial and brought it up to her nose. She sniffed cautiously.

"I don't know," she said, frowning a little. "You can still smell something, even after all this time, but I can't tell—"

Nellie reached for the vial. She gave it a quick sniff.

"It's mace," she said immediately. "That spice I bought. The outer covering of a nutmeg."

The three of them beamed at one another.

"A clue and the next location, both inside about thirty seconds!" Dan crowed.

The man in gray was standing behind Nellie. They had been so engrossed in the box and its contents, none of them had noticed when he rejoined them.

"Well done," he said quietly.

He sat down and took off his sunglasses. Then, to Amy's astonishment, he wiped his eyes as if they were tearing up.

He cleared his throat and picked up the box. "Made by a renegade Ekat," he said. "Most ingenious, wouldn't you say? The Ekaterinas claimed this area—the Caribbean—long ago and have been very active here. By the way, I thought you would like to know that your cat is safe in Kingston. We will collect him when we leave here."

He put the box back on the table. "I must apologize," he said. "First, for my earlier unpleasantness. As you will learn shortly, it was all part of the grand scheme.

And second, because I've never properly introduced myself. My name is Fiske Cahill. And I would like to thank you for bringing such joy to my sister."

His sister?

"Grace," he said as he sat down next to Nellie. "Grace was my sister."

Amy's jaw dropped.

Grace had one sibling—Aunt Beatrice. Neither of them had ever once mentioned a brother. It couldn't be true!

"How come we never heard of you?" Dan asked.

The man winced and slumped a little in his chair. "There is no easy answer to that question," he said, almost to himself. He paused and took a breath. "As a small child, I was painfully shy. So much so that I simply couldn't function when I was with other people. My parents allowed me to stay out of school, at home with a tutor. Perhaps that was a mistake because in the end, it made it easier for me to—to disappear altogether when I decided as a young man that I wanted nothing to do with—with the family business."

He gave them a searching look, and Amy knew what business he meant: the hunt for the 39 Clues.

The man laced his fingers together and stared at his hands. "As children, Grace and I adored each other. She was the only one I kept in touch with over the years, and on my terms, not hers. I would call or write once in a while, brief visits every other year or so. It was not until she became ill that I went to see her for an extended time."

He shook his head, and his already soft voice lowered to a whisper. "Of the many poor choices I made in my life, the one I most regret is not spending more time with her."

Amy felt her throat clutch a little. What would it be like if Dan disappeared from her life? Then she caught herself and frowned. If Fiske Cahill wasn't telling the truth, he was an awfully good actor. He probably wanted her to think exactly what she had been thinking. She had to stay on guard. . . .

"I hope that is sufficient explanation as to why you have never heard of me," he was saying, "because there is no other. Grace, in her last days, asked me to become involved in the hunt for clues. I could not refuse her."

"Not good enough," Dan said. "You still haven't given us any real proof that you're Grace's brother."

Fiske Cahill sat in silence for a moment. Then he lifted his chin, blinked his eyes, and spoke in a nasal, high-pitched voice. "Anyone who plays this silly game is a fool. I'll take the money!"

Amy stared at him in amazement. He had just done a pitch-perfect imitation of Aunt Beatrice!

Aunt Beatrice had said something almost exactly

like that on the day Grace's will was read. The mimicry was dead-on. It could only have been done by someone who knew her well — *very* well.

"You were there?" Amy whispered.

"Yes. Hidden, and listening from another room. My oldest sister's voice can be quite irritating, as of course you know."

Amy looked at Dan. He gave her a combined nod and shrug.

She shook her head in response. "It could still be a trick," she said. "He could have, like, studied her. You know, followed her around like a stalker, or filmed her, or something like that. And practiced imitating her. Or maybe he's working on some kind of plot with her —"

"With *Beatrice*?" Fiske Cahill said.

"With *Aunt Beatrice*?" Dan said.

Not only had they spoken at the same moment, but they had identical incredulous expressions on their faces. Amy was struck by a revelation. For so long, she had heard about how much she reminded people of Grace. Miss Alice had recognized their resemblance to each other even though she hadn't seen Grace in years. Now Amy saw precisely the same kind of likeness between Dan and the man in gray!

They had to be related.

CHAPTER 22

"I have so much to tell you, I hardly know where to start," Fiske Cahill said. "I will do my best. You already know that you are Madrigals."

"Yeah, and we know that's bad news," Dan said.

"Not necessarily," Fiske replied. "It depends on your point of view."

"Oh, great," Dan said, "now everything's much clearer."

For a split second, Amy thought Fiske might smile. But then his eyebrows drew together and he looked very serious.

"Gideon and Olivia Cahill had four children," Fiske said. He paused, waiting.

Dan and Amy looked at each other. Apparently, this was sort of a quiz.

"Katherine, Luke, Thomas, and Jane," Amy said.

Fiske nodded his approval. "Gideon spent a fortune and a lifetime trying to find a cure for the plague. The serum he created did indeed protect against the plague, and also had unexpected side effects.

Although he didn't know it at the time, his serum altered the DNA of those who took it, giving them greater abilities in every area of human endeavor. Eventually, Gideon gave each of his children part of the formula. Soon afterwards, he died in a fire that destroyed his laboratory. His children suspected one another of sabotage, which sundered the family. Each child went off to spearhead a particular branch of the Cahill clan."

Pause.

Dan's turn. "Ekaterina, Lucian, Tomas, Janus."

Another nod. "For centuries now, the branches have been on a relentless search, battling one another to find clues to the ingredients that will reconstruct the formula, both their own particular serum and the master serum that contains the secret to the powers of all four branches. But every time a branch comes close, they are prevented from achieving success."

"By the Madrigals," Amy whispered.

"So that's why all the other branches hate them—I mean, us," Dan said. "But how did the Madrigals get mixed up with the clue hunt in the first place?"

Fiske answered the question with one of his own. "Amy," he said, "may I see that miniature painting?"

Puzzled, Amy took the painting out of her backpack and handed it to him.

He gazed at it for a few moments, then spoke slowly. "At the time of the fire, no one knew that Gideon's wife, Olivia, was pregnant with their fifth child."

He turned the painting around so it was facing them.

"Meet Madeleine Cahill," he said. "Founder of the Madrigal line."

Amy had looked at the little painting dozens of times before, but it was as if she were seeing it for the first time. It was incredible — no wonder the woman in the picture was a dead ringer for her mother!

"Your great-great — well, about twenty-two greats — grandmother," Fiske said.

"She's the one who wrote the poem," Dan said, gesturing at the box. "MC. Madeleine Cahill."

Fiske nodded as he put the painting down gently. He cleared his throat. "Olivia Cahill supported her husband's efforts at first," he said, "when he was trying to find a cure for the plague. But she was devastated by what the obsession with the serum's side effects did to the family. Her children scattered across the globe to begin their own schemes. She was left alone with the baby.

"Olivia was terrified of the corrupting power of the serum. She also desperately wanted to bring the family together again, and she raised Madeleine to believe that nothing was more important."

Amy made a small noise of surprise. Her face lit up, not in happiness, but in understanding.

Fiske Cahill cracked his first smile. "Why don't you go ahead, young lady?"

"That's in the poem, too!" Amy burst out. "One web, many a tether, united—that's what the Madrigals do! They try to get the other branches to stop fighting!"

"Exactly," Fiske said.

"I don't get it," Dan said crossly. "If you ask me, they sure don't act like peacekeepers a lot of the time."

Fiske looked solemn again. "I'm afraid you're right, Dan. Preventing the branches from achieving too much power has not always been a pleasant task. And just as important, the Madrigals try to protect innocent people from becoming victims of the battle."

"Oh. Ah." Dan was momentarily struck speechless, and Amy knew he was trying to wrap his mind around the same thoughts she was having.

The Madrigals—they're the good guys*? But how—*

"The other branches would be most unhappy to learn that the Madrigals have equal status as Cahill heirs and even more unhappy if they knew what the Madrigal quest was," Fiske continued. "That is why the branch has always been shrouded in secrecy."

"And—and Mom and Dad?" Amy asked. "That's what they were doing, too?"

Fiske nodded. "They were among our most active members. Something else you should know: The Lucians pinned the blame for one of their own evil acts on Hope and Arthur. It happened in South Africa."

Winnie Thembeka! Amy's mind flashed back to the terrible moment when she and Dan had been told that their parents were murderers.

"I knew it! I knew they were good all along!" Dan exulted as he held his fist out toward Amy.

Amy returned his fist bump, but inside she didn't feel quite the same triumph as her brother. *They had to make hard choices, too,* she thought. *Being good might seem simple, but it's never easy.*

"What about Austria?" Dan asked. "Was that all part of the plan, too—to blow us up? Then what, rescue us? Pretty risky if you ask me—we could have died!"

"It was Alistair Oh who triggered the explosion," Fiske said. "Believe me, we were relieved beyond words to learn that you were safe. You assumed that I was the culprit, and we decided it would be useful not to correct that assumption. It reinforced the image of Madrigal power among those in the other branches."

Now Nellie spoke up. "You two scared me to death when you said you wanted out of the hunt," she said. "I knew how much the Madrigals needed you."

Fiske nodded solemnly. "Without the Madrigals working at full strength, there would be countless people who would meet a fate like Lester's," he said gently. "Who knows how many more . . ."

The fate of the world, Amy thought.

There was quiet around the table. Amy saw that some of the hurt had returned to Dan's eyes but not the empty hurt like before. Instead, she saw a kind of determination there. No one else would die like Lester had, not if Dan could help it.

She was with him on that one.

It was Dan who broke the silence.

"There's one thing I still don't get," he said. "Why couldn't we have known all this before? Why did Mr. McIntyre tell us to *beware* the Madrigals? Why couldn't Grace have told us we were Madrigals and what the Madrigals do?"

Fiske sighed. "That is, perhaps, the most complicated part of the equation," he said. "Madeleine Cahill swore an oath on her mother's deathbed to do everything in her power to reunite the family. She was well aware of how difficult the Madrigals' task would be and spent years designing and implementing guidelines for the branch.

"Some of these you already know, even if you don't know you know them. The Madrigal branch is matrilineal—Madrigals often take the last name of their mothers, not their fathers. It was a symbol of Madeleine's devotion to Olivia."

"So that's why we're Cahills and not Trents," Dan said.

"Mom always told me it was a feminist thing," Amy recalled.

Dan thought for a moment. "That wasn't really a lie," he said.

"But most important," Fiske continued, "Madeleine knew that the only chance for success was if the Madrigals themselves were the best of the best. Amelia Earhart, as you discovered. Anne Bonny, Mary Read, Nanny Sharpe. All Madrigals. Many more names—Mother Teresa, Frederick Douglass, Roberto Clemente. And more than half of the Nobel Peace Prize winners."

"Wow." That was Amy and Dan, together.

"There's more," Fiske went on. "The Madrigal line is the only one of the Cahill branches for which active status must be *earned.* Simply being born into the line is not enough."

"Earned?" Dan said. "Earned how?"

"Cahills who exhibit the potential to become active Madrigals have to undergo a period of rigorous trials, *without knowing they are doing so.* That way, if they do not succeed, the secret of the Madrigal line remains inviolate.

"Some of the trials result from conflict with the other branches or from the hunt itself. Others are—how can I put it—designed by the Madrigals themselves. This last challenge was actually a combination. We needed the fang and hoped fervently that you could obtain it. Once you had achieved that, we decided you should be put to the test of opening the box under rather menacing conditions."

"So the Madrigals have deliberately been trying to trip us up all along?" Dan's voice rose higher, on the edge of anger.

"They have also given you aid from time to time," Fiske shot back. "Believe me, we want all the active members we can get. We *want* you to succeed. But we cannot let our desires get in the way of our goal to select only the most worthy.

"The activities of potential Madrigals are tracked

quite closely, hence, Miss Gomez's involvement. And the need for her deception."

"I'm sorry, guys," Nellie said. "I wanted to tell you about a million times, but—"

Then Nellie put her head down on the table, and a moment later, Amy could hear strange snuffling noises.

What the heck—is she—no, it can't be—

"Are you *crying*?" Dan asked, staring at Nellie in amazement.

Nellie raised her tear-streaked face to Amy. "It was s-so awful," she said. "H-having to lie to you, and—and then when you f-found out, you didn't trust me anymore, it was almost like you hated me—and—and I had to keep g-going somehow—" She put her head down again, shaking with sobs.

For a long moment, Amy felt almost blind with anger. Part of her wanted to hit something or someone as hard as she could—for putting the three of them through all this.

Nellie had indeed betrayed them. Many times over—to Mr. McIntyre, to the man in black, to the Madrigals.

But she had done it for the right reasons. And it couldn't have been easy.

Amy took a deep breath. She exhaled slowly, trying to blow away all of her anger.

It worked. Mostly, anyway.

When her vision cleared, she found herself staring at

Nellie's spiky blond-and-black hair . . . tough-as-nails Nellie, reduced to a puddle by the Clue hunt. . . .

She reached out and put her hand on Nellie's arm. "Nellie?" she said softly. "I'm sorry, too. Really sorry. It must have been so hard for you."

"Yeah, Nellie," Dan said, his voice anxious. "Everything's cool now, so you can quit bawling, okay?"

The snuffling noises grew quieter. Fiske cleared his throat. "Miss Gomez was not always as cooperative as we would have liked," he said. "There were a number of times when she acted against our wishes. Helping you with Isabel Kabra earlier, for example. And just now with the box."

Nellie sat up, sniffed loudly, and scrubbed at her tears, leaving mascara tracks in interesting designs all over her cheeks.

"What you gonna do," she said, and managed a watery wink at Amy.

Amy winked back.

It was amazing how the tiny twitch of an eyelid could give her such a huge feeling of relief.

"Indeed." Fiske seemed almost amused. Then he went on again. "After the designated trial period, those who are deemed worthy are notified of their active Madrigal status, and the secrets of the Madrigal line are revealed to them."

Amy drew in a sharp breath. "So if you're telling us all this now—"

Fiske Cahill nodded.

"Yes. I have been authorized to tell you both, Amy and Dan, that you have been granted active Madrigal status." He paused. "I might add, you are by far the youngest candidates ever to have achieved this."

Amy was pretty sure his eyes were watering again.

"Your grandmother would be so proud of you," he said. "As am I."

Dan bounced in his chair. "Is there, like, a certificate? Or a pin or a badge or something?"

Fiske smiled and inclined his head. "Sorry, nothing like that. But there is a reward of a different sort—"

He stopped and glanced around furtively. "As of today, seven Madrigal clues have been discovered," he said. "Mace, of course, thanks to your good selves. Also—" he leaned toward them and whispered the other Clues quickly but clearly.

I should try to remember them all, Amy thought. Just then, Dan elbowed her gently and nodded. She knew what that meant. *He's already got them memorized.*

"With this knowledge comes a great responsibility," Fiske said. "The Cahill clan must be reunited. It was Grace's greatest desire; she spent her lifetime preparing for it. It's why she wrote her will the way she did: to trigger the hunt for the thirty-nine clues. She hoped the hunt would prove so difficult that the clans would band together to complete it."

He paused and looked at each of them in turn.

"As you well know, that hasn't happened. The hunt is nearly over now. England will be our last chance. Your focus there will be twofold: to win the clue hunt for the Madrigal branch, and even more important, to bring the family together."

"The family?" Amy said, confused. Who was he talking about—him and Aunt Beatrice?

"Yes," Fiske said. "The other Cahill branches. You must work with them, get them to cooperate, and trust you and one another. It will be the most difficult challenge you have ever faced."

Amy could hardly believe what she was hearing. Winning the Clue race would be hard enough, but to get all four branches to cooperate?

The feuding, lying, treacherous Wizards and Ohs and Holts?

And worst of all . . .

"Isabel?" Dan screeched in alarm. "You expect us to work with *her*? No way—never in a million years!"

"We c-couldn't," Amy stuttered. "Our parents, she—they—we—"

Fiske lowered his head. "I knew your mother as a girl," he said softly. "A terrible loss, for one so bright to die so young. And the same for your father."

Another silence. Then Fiske cleared his throat.

"Tell me," he said, "what do you think they would want you to do?"

How many times had Amy wondered that herself? Would her parents want her to stay out of trouble—to be safe and to keep Dan safe? Maybe . . . but how safe could they ever be in a world run by someone like Isabel? How safe would anyone be?

Dan pushed back his chair and stood up. Amy could see that his mind was made up, and she knew he was right.

Not revenge, she thought again. *Justice. And not just for us and our parents, but for the whole world.*

"We better get going," Dan said. "England! But first we pick up Saladin, and then"—his voice grew quieter—"then we have to go see Miss Alice."

They were all quiet for a few moments.

Amy felt her heart breaking when she thought of Miss Alice, how lonely she would be without Lester.

"The Madrigals will help her, financially and otherwise," Fiske said. "Now, and for the rest of her life."

Lester would like that, Amy thought. *If only we could do more for her somehow. . . .*

"And," Fiske said, "they have made another decision. For the first time in their history, the Madrigals are granting active status to someone *not* born to the bloodline."

He turned to Nellie.

"Miss Gomez? Welcome to the Madrigals."

Amy watched as the expression on Nellie's face went from confusion to astonishment to pleasure. Then she blushed a very rosy pink.

"*Dude,*" she said.